Blackwing Defender

ISBN-13: 978-1537579818
ISBN-10: 1537579819
Copyright © 2016, T. S. Joyce
First electronic publication: September 2016

T. S. Joyce
www.tsjoyce.com

All Rights Are Reserved. No part of this book may be used or reproduced in any manner whatsoever without written permission, except in the case of brief quotations embodied in critical articles and reviews. The unauthorized reproduction or distribution of this copyrighted work is illegal. No part of this book may be scanned, uploaded or distributed via the Internet or any other means, electronic or print, without the author's permission.

NOTE FROM THE AUTHOR:

This book is a work of fiction. The names, characters, places, and incidents are products of the writer's imagination or have been used fictitiously and are not to be construed as real. Any resemblance to persons, living or dead, actual events, locale or organizations is entirely coincidental. The author does not have any control over and does not assume any responsibility for third-party websites or their content.

Published in the United States of America

First digital publication: September 2016
First print publication: September 2016

Editing: Corinne DeMaagd
Cover Photography: Kruse Images & Photography
Cover Model: BT Urruela

Blackwing Defender

(Kane's Mountains, Book 1)

T. S. JOYCE

DEDICATION

For my dog/fur baby/buddy for life, Oscar, who keeps me company during all the long work hours. And who also just farted and smelled up my entire office as I was writing this dedication to him. Oscar, you smell, but you're still my best bud.

ACKNOWLEDGMENTS

I couldn't write these books without my amazing team behind me. A huge thanks to Corinne DeMaagd, for helping me to polish my books, and for being an amazing and supportive friend. And to the wonderful photog and model I worked with on this book. Shauna Kruse and BT Urruela came through big-time on the exact shot I'd asked for, and I adore them infinitely for the effort. And to my man and our two cubs, who put up with a lot of crazy work hours from me and take everything in stride. It takes a special group of supporters to cheer something like this on, day in and day out, and they never waver on it.

And last but never least, thank you, awesome reader. You have done more for me and my stories than I can even explain on this teeny page. You found my books, and ran with them, and every share, review, and comment makes release days so incredibly special to me. 1010 is magic and so are you.

ONE

Mornings here were unlike anything Winter Donovan had ever seen. She'd been born and raised a city shifter, but then everything had gone sideways and she'd landed in the middle of nowhere, in the Red Havoc Crew. Kind of. She wasn't an official member, but she could be if she wanted.

It was minutes before dawn, the ones where the sky was still navy and dotted with stars. The moon was low and looked tired, and on the horizon the dark blue faded to gray where the sky kissed the earth.

Today would be the worst day of her life.

She smelled him before she saw him, and her body reacted, the traitor. A wave of excitement took her before she remembered, but that one second of hopefulness made the devastation even deeper.

Brody strode out of the shadows, his face somber. It didn't suit him. He'd always been a happy man, or perhaps just with the others. With her, his lips thinned into a grim line, and his soft green eyes pooled with pity. She'd fallen in love with those eyes. There was something to that old saying about the eyes being the windows to the soul.

Brody used to have a beautiful soul.

He sank down beside her as she avoided the hell out of his gaze and tied her hiking boot.

"You going for a walk?" he asked, ripping up a blade of grass.

More like an all-day hike through the wilderness. "Yeah, I'm not exactly invited to the party today." She wished she could help the bitterness in her voice, but she couldn't.

"Probably best you aren't around."

She huffed a heartbroken breath at the pain his words caused. "Why are you here? You haven't talked to me in a month, and now you're here to what? Break more of me? Hurt me until I can't climb out of the goddamned hole you put me in?"

"I'm here to say I'm sorry."

She stared at him, utterly shocked. He looked like he wanted to retch, and she understood that feeling. She'd had it ever since he'd gotten Lynn pregnant.

"You don't think this apology came way too late, Brody? I've waited for this for the last five months, and you denied me. You never admitted you were wrong, and here I've sat, pushed to the outer edge of the crew, pushed away from you, from the others. This was supposed to be my day, Brody. I was supposed to wear white and pledge to you, but you gave it to her behind my back."

"Well, you'll have to move on—"

"To who, Brody?" She hated him. She hated the pathetic woman he'd molded her into. "No one in Red Havoc calls to my bond like you, and now I have to watch you with her, day in, day out. Laughing, kissing, touching. I guess I'm supposed to be glad you've found happiness, but I thought you were happy with me."

"I was, but it's different with Lynn." Brody shrugged, and his puppy-dog eyes begged her understanding. "It's just...better."

Pissed at the streaming tears that dampened her cheeks, Winter stomped her boot on the ground and slammed her back against the stair behind her. *Better.* Story of her life.

She was the best at being second place.

Brody buried his face in his hands and sniffed hard as if he actually had a heart. "This wasn't how it was supposed to be," he murmured in a cracking voice. "We were practically made for each other. You were supposed to be it, and then I…I don't know…my animal just picked someone different… Fuck, Winter, I'm sorry."

"Please leave," she said, her face angled away to hide her pain. He didn't deserve to see how hard this was on her.

He rested his fingertips on her shoulder, but she jerked out from under his touch. His comfort was for Lynn now.

Brody sniffed again and stood. As he walked away, Winter forced herself not to watch him go. She was better than that, but not quite good enough to wish him a happy wedding day. She could tell when he'd gone, though, because his scent was replaced by another. It was replaced by Benson Saber's.

"Alpha," she whispered in a shaky voice as she exposed her neck.

Ben sat down beside her. "No use calling me that, Winter Girl. You and I both know you won't be pledging to my crew now." He handed her a metal flask.

Winter frowned at his offering. "It's six in the morning."

When Ben arched his ruddy eyebrow, she gave in, took it from his hand, unscrewed the cap, and took a long, burning drag. The alpha of Red Havoc liked whiskey.

"Remember when you first came to me?" he asked, his attention on the woods.

"Yeah, you were so lucky to land me."

Ben snorted. "You were such a little shit, and stubborn. Tough." He cast her a gold-eyed glance. "Broken."

"And three years later, and I'm the same damn person."

"No. You're different. You met Brody a few days in, and you used him as your anchor. You got your shit together for him, but maybe that was the problem, Winter. You didn't do it for you." Ben pulled a folded piece of paper from his back pocket and handed it to her. "This was posted on Air Ryder Croy's social media late last night."

Winter handed him the flask and took the paper, unfolded it, and read silently.

New Crew Announcement:

Dark Kane, the mother fuckin' demon dragon himself and my fourth best friend will be holding interviews for his Blackwing Crew on September 21. Be there or be a boring asshole, makes no difference to me. Wear short shorts for bonus points. Come ready to party.

Love and Penises,
Air Ryder

Realization blasted through her, and she shot Ben a horrified glance. "You're kicking me out of Red Havoc?"

"Winter, you were never Red Havoc, and you know it. I wanted you to be. I waited for you to tell me you were ready to pledge, but you never pulled the trigger. And I can see your future if you stay here. You're so fuckin' loyal. Your heart latches onto someone and doesn't let them go. Brody's moving on, but you won't. You can't when you're this close to him. You'll watch him with Lynn, watch him as a newlywed, watch them bring that little panther into the world, watch him parent, and wish it was all happening to you. You'll regress to that little shit that came to me three years ago begging a place to stay for a night. Your story doesn't end here, Winter. This was just a bump in the road."

"But with the dragons?" she whispered. She'd seen the battle in the sky between Dark Kane and his mate, Rowan. They were monstrous and had burned the Smoky Mountains. Winter was just a panther shifter and no match for a crew of fire-breathers.

"Listen, Kane's hard. He's intimidating. He's quiet and tough, but he was my friend once, and deep down, he's one of the good ones. If Kane is setting up a crew, I want you in it. Do you understand? You'll be safe under the dragon's wing."

"Like I was safe here?" she rasped, clutching the paper to her chest. She'd come here for sanctuary, but somehow Brody had made her trust even less.

"This ain't me choosing Brody over you. I want to claw him a dozen times a day for what he and Lynn did to you. This is me saying it's okay to move on and get back on the right path." Benson ran his hand roughly over his cropped hair and stood. "Pack your shit, Winter. You're gonna do big things someday. Just not here."

Ben turned away fast and strode off, but she'd seen it. She'd seen the alpha's eyes were rimmed with moisture. This hurt him, too. He'd been her friend. He'd invested a lot into pulling her from the brink. He'd refused to put her down when he probably should have, and now he was admitting he couldn't do anything more for her. It hurt deep in her chest, but not because she was being pushed out.

It hurt most because Ben was the strongest man she'd ever known, and he was admitting defeat with her.

Just like everyone else did.

TWO

Winter cast a quick glance at the surveillance camera camouflaged in the branches of a white pine. It was aimed right at the full mailbox and dirt-road entry to Dark Kane's territory. Someone was paranoid.

Right now, the dragon was probably sitting in his big, fancy cliff mansion sipping his Bloody Mary or whatever the fuck fancy people drank and watching as she drove her junky old two-seater truck past the No Trespassing sign. She missed Red Havoc already. Not Brody, though. Brody could sit on a tack with his ball sack.

The road dropped steeply. The angle was so harsh she had a moment of panic when the road disappeared from under her, and she had to trust the truck to dive nose-first down the gravel lane. It wasn't so bad once she got over that first drop-off, but the road curved this way and that. Dark Kane had picked one mountainous, treacherous territory. One last curve through the forest, and a small bridge appeared. She gasped and jerked her truck to a stop behind a green Mustang with black racing stripes. There were cars jammed all along the road as far as she could see and parked between trees in the woods.

"What the fuck?" she muttered, squinting at a pair of giant men making their way over the one-lane bridge. Up ahead, another trio of bright-eyed shifters cast her a calculating glance over their shoulders, then disappeared into the woods.

She fought the urge to throw her truck in reverse and escape this place. The dragons were bad, but being in a small territory with a bunch of other shifters when her panther wasn't the most dominant creature on the planet would've normally been a hell no.

Get back on the right path. She could hear Ben's voice so clearly, as if he sat in the seat next to her, telling her not to chicken out. Her options were limited. Go back to Red Havoc and accept the pain that would always sit on her heart, or cast her net for happiness a little wider.

Clearly, she wouldn't be accepted in the Blackwing Crew if there were so many to choose from, so what could it hurt to spend the day seeing what was what? At least she wasn't in Red Havoc, hiding in her cabin with her music blaring as Brody and Lynn honeymoon fucked—loudly—two doors down.

If nothing else, the Smoky Mountains were beautiful. She hadn't even known a place this stunning existed just a six-hour drive away from Ben's crew. The trees stretched up to the sky, and the ground alongside the road was covered in ivy, moss, and ferns. What sky she could see through the thick canopy was such a vibrant blue, it was breathtaking.

Mind made up, she shoved her door open and didn't bother locking it because she was the only one who knew the tricks to get old Rusty started. It was burglar proof, and besides, if she locked it, she might not be able to get back in without climbing through the sliding rear window. The lock was touchy. She liked that old Rusty was such an asshole, though.

Winter caught a glimpse of herself in the window and froze. She looked sad. Somber. Her eyes were tired and empty, and her mouth was set in such a grim line she couldn't even see a hint of the dimples that usually sat on her cheeks. Or used to sit there before Brody slowly sucked the light from her. Her black hair hung limply around her shoulders, the honey-colored highlights half grown out. No make-up, no expression, she was a ghost of her former self. Winter ripped her gaze away from the reflection and made her way to the bridge. She avoided mirrors, and this was why. The bottomless disappointment in herself was soul-wracking. She should've never given Brody power over her. Ben was right in that she was too damn loyal, and Brody, the cheating rat, hadn't ever earned that kind of devotion.

She shouldered her purse and made tracks in the gravel to put space between her and the ghost reflection.

There was arguing up ahead in the woods. In the center of a loose circle of muscled-up shifters, there were two men pummeling each other's faces. And they were smiling, the psychopaths. Typical dominant shifter shit. Winter rolled her eyes and kept trekking. The river flowing under the bridge made a pretty sound that combatted the noises of grunts and snarls. She made her way up the winding gravel road, but as she hit a steep incline, her boots slipped on the loose rocks.

She trailed the pair of shifters she'd seen earlier. They seemed to know where they were going, and really, there was only one road. The interviews were probably being held in the lair of the dragons. Just the thought blasted chills across her arms. Winter had watched the news footage of their battle a dozen times at least. Kane had a suppressed dragon, and when his mate Rowan had set it free, they'd gone to war and leveled the surrounding mountains with fire. It had been a few months, but still, she could smell the lingering smoke that had saturated the Smoky Mountains.

They were enormous beasts, and Kane's black dragon looked like some ancient scarred-up monster with gargoyle wings. Rowan Barnett's gray dragon was much smaller. She was sleek and beautiful, but a ripper, apparent from the way she'd dragged Kane's dragon into the clouds, slashing and biting and spraying him with fire and lava. When they'd crashed back down to earth, the tourist who had been videoing the battle was rocketed backward against a tree with the force, and the footage had cut out.

And here was Winter, waltzing into the territory of the deadliest beasts that inhabited the earth. Maybe she had a death wish. Or maybe dying by dragon's fire would still be better than ripping her own goddamn heart out every time she saw Brody lean in to kiss Lynn. She didn't know why, but she didn't even have nervous flutters as she made her way into a clearing. She just felt numb, like she wasn't really here, and this was all a dream. Her life had been planned in Red Havoc. Marriage, cubs, happily ever after, yet here she stood in the shadow of a towering yellow buckeye tree, hoping for the chance to change her stars, while forty shifters milled about the yard in front of a small cabin, hoping for the same.

Meandering on the parameter wouldn't get her close to the dragons, so she picked her way through the crowd. Her senses were overwhelmed with the smells and snarls of animals as she passed. Fur and dominance mingled to make the air thick like water in her lungs. Holding her breath, she dipped her gaze to the ground and put one foot in front of the other until she reached a circle of logs that surrounded a fire pit to the left of the cabin.

"Girl," said a lithe looking man with sandy-blond, shoulder-length hair from his seat on a log. "Pay up asshole, there are three now. Told you this wasn't going to be a boy's club."

A stocky man with piercings all down one ear and blazing blue eyes slapped a ten-dollar bill in the man's hand and spat on the dirt near Winter's feet. He stood and brushed by her, bumping her hard in the shoulder as though it was her fault he made a bad bet. He smelled like a bear shifter.

She hissed before she could stop herself.

"Whoa, down kitty," Long Hair said.

When she dragged her pissed-off attention back to him, she froze. His eyes were bi-colored, one blue and one seafoam green, both glowing. Despite his smile, whatever animal he harbored was just as worked up as hers. "You're in luck, kitty cat. A seat just happened to open up. It's all warmed up for you and everything." He twitched his head toward the bear's empty spot then offered her a bright smile. "He was a farter."

When some of the others chuckled, Winter looked around the circle. There were, in fact, two other females, one in all black with smeared mascara and a foundation three shades too light. Her dyed black hair was up in pigtails, and her lipstick matched the dark hue of her messy tresses. Winter would've assumed her a vampire if it wasn't broad daylight. Next to her was a honey-haired beauty who looked frail as a mouse and wore hearing aids. She was scribbling something into a journal and ignored the scuffle that was happening right behind her. Sitting on her other side was a giant the size of a Viking ship with broad shoulders, a buzzed head, and tattoos down his arms. His profile was to her, but as if he felt her studying him, he turned and locked gazes with her. A tiny gasp left her lips before she hurried across the fire pit next to Long Hair. The beastly giant was still staring at her. He had a neatly trimmed blond beard, pretty blue eyes, and a straight nose. Perfect, full lips, too, but someone, or something, had ruined his symmetrical features by raking its claws down the side of his face and scarring him to hell. The man's eyes tightened at the corners, and then he turned on his log and gave her his massive back.

She scented the air, but they all smelled terrifying. No way in hell could she differentiate between their smells now. The fine hairs on the back of her neck were standing straight up, and when she settled onto the log, it only got worse. She'd sandwiched herself between Long Hair and a man she hadn't even noticed before. He was a huge shadow in her senses. The kind that screamed for her not to turn and look him directly in the eye. Oh, he was a bear, of that she was sure. A grizzly likely, and she'd accepted the wrong damn seat.

"Breathe," the man murmured, the sound of his voice gravel and silk.

Winter gripped her jeans at the knees and sat there panting, wishing she could stand and leave without giving any of these psychos her back.

With a sigh, the man stood. And stood and stood because he was as tall as a mountain. "Don't show anybody your neck, kitty. You don't have an alpha here. Not yet."

As he walked to the other side and gave her some space, she straightened her neck back out, shook her head hard, and sucked in a deep breath of relief. Two of the men across the circle inched away from the monster bear and then stood and slunk away from him completely. He was massive, but not in the physical sense. He felt everywhere, as if he took up every air molecule, every inch of space, and she hadn't even looked at his face yet. How had he been the last one she noticed? How had he hidden until she'd sat down beside him? There was nothing more terrifying than a monster so easily disguised.

She could see him out of her peripheral, could feel him watching her, but fuck if she was going to be the prey. Swallowing down her yellow-bellied fear, Winter dragged her gaze to his. She froze at the breathtaking, masculine beauty of the man. Tall, yes, broad shouldered, yes, but his face gave her such an odd sense of déjà vu, even though she'd never laid eyes on him in her life. She would've remembered. His hair was dark brown, matching the scruff on his chiseled jaw. It was his eyes that held her though—dark, broody, hard, seeming to take in everything with a glance. Right now, he could've been looking straight through to her soul. His dark brows lowered slightly, and he took a step back, angled his chin down, and looked at her suspiciously. "Do I know you?" he asked in that deep velvet voice of his.

Winter forced her attention anywhere else other than his mesmerizing eyes. It was cool outside, but the man wore a dark gray T-shirt with forest green writing too faded to read the logo. Black tattoo ink trailed down one arm, while the other was bare and tan as though he'd spent a lot of time outdoors. He crossed his arms over his defined chest and murmured, "I'm Logan."

Logan. He even had a sexpot name. It was perfect for a man who was pretending to be normal when his inner animal clearly was not. More camouflage.

"Winter," she said with a nod.

"Winter?" Logan asked. "You a snow leopard?"

She huffed an uncomfortable breath. The real story was her mom was probably high as a kite when she named a black panther cub Winter. These strangers hadn't earned real stories though, so they could have the surface one instead—the one Mom had told her when she'd been slumped over in a corner with a needle hanging out of her arm. "I was born during a blizzard. So…Winter."

"Names?" Long Hair asked. "We're finally doing introductions? We've been sitting here for three hours, and it takes this haggard-lookin' chick to get us to open up."

The giant scar-faced man beside him snarled and snapped his teeth at Long Hair like a psychopath, but the smaller man only ducked out of the way and lifted two fingers. "Dustin Porter, the next and best member of the Blackwing Crew."

The goth girl snorted and leaned back on locked arms. "Look around, Fido. The dragons aren't going to choose everyone. They'll pick ten, maybe. Hate to be the one to crush your dreams, but you wouldn't make the shortlist."

"Fido? So you guessed what I am... What are you? Make an actual introduction, Princess Emo, *or* I can guess all the animals here. I'm good at this." Dustin sniffed the air and jerked his attention to the goliath beside him. "You're a werepussy for sure."

The giant let off a low rumble and neatly collected Dustin's neck in his clenched fist.

"Pussy as in a cat! A big cat shifter," Dustin wheezed out, then gasped as the titan released him. "Fuck," he muttered rubbing his throat. "You almost popped my head off like a champagne cork."

The giant curled his lips back over his teeth and offered Dustin a feral look before he gave them all his back again. "People call me Beast. And fuck your labels. You don't know me."

There was a loaded moment of silence before Logan saved them all from the awkwardness. "I'm a bear."

"Yeah, I think we could all tell that," Winter muttered.

"Not her," Dustin said, pointing to the quiet girl with the hearing aids. "She smells pretty fuckin' human to me. Here for a pity-bite, love? I don't think the dragon will stand for it."

"Hey, she could be a flight shifter," the goth girl said.

"Emma, human," the girl clarified carefully in a thick voice. She rolled her fist, flipped off Dustin, and then went back to scribbling in her journal after she fiddled with the little device on her right ear.

"Did you just turn off your hearing aid?" Dustin asked in an offended tone.

Winter snorted. She liked the human already.

When she looked up at Logan, he was showing the first signs of a smile. She bet the monster was beautiful when he let a real grin rip.

A car horn blasted, and the crowd parted like the

red sea as a jacked-up pickup truck approached. One redheaded muscle-bound titan was yelling out the window, "Out the way before I run you over!" Air Ryder Croy pointed to some brownnoser who had actually worn cut-off shorts for extra points. "I like your shorts. Move! Oh, wait!" He rocked to a stop and leaned farther into his truck, then reappeared at the open window and flung a stack of papers into the air. They rained down like giant white snowflakes. "Applications! Fill them out! Oh, here's a pen." He chucked a single pen out the window into the surging crowd.

"One pen, seriously?" someone yelled.

"Crew shit 101—learn to share," Air Ryder called out over the noise as he began inching his truck toward the cabin again.

Logan cast Winter an unreadable glance. His eyes had lightened from pitch black to smoke gray. "I'll get the applications." The rest in the circle had stood, including Winter, urged by the chaos of the mob scrambling for the fluttering papers, but true to his word, Logan brought back a stack in less time than Winter had expected. They took them as he passed them around the circle. All but the giant scar-faced bruiser, Beast. He snarled and stood, disappeared into the crowd, and returned thirty seconds later with his own. A team player he was not.

She thought he would stay on the other side where he'd been standing, but Logan handed her an application and took his seat beside her again. "You sure got a big purse," he said. "Any extra pens in there?"

"Yeah," she said on a breath as she dug around the depths of her oversize handbag. She carried everything in it—way more than she needed. There was even a pair of purple hand wraps for boxing, a back scratcher, and four pocket knives. Like she needed all those weapons. She had teeth and claws.

Winter found three pens and tossed Emma one since she was looking right at her like a brave little human. Dustin snorted a disapproving sound, but so what? He smelled like dog fur, and she wouldn't ever go out of her way to help a werewolf. They were crazy and manipulative, every last one of them. It was ingrained in them since birth. He might be acting normal, but he wasn't. That was just a show to play nice and try to get into Kane's crew.

The other pen, she handed to Logan. His

fingertip brushed hers as he took it, but he didn't flinch away from her touch. He sat there, frowning down at her, linked to her by the pen and this tiny brush of skin.

"These questions are bullshit," a shifter yelled from behind her. "How many times do you jack off a day? Would you consider yourself a sexual delinquent? And they aren't yes or no questions, but a scale from one to fifty!"

Winter giggled when she read the first one. Clearly, Air Ryder had put this application together himself. Instead of asking *Male or Female* it said *Dick or Treasure Cavern*.

Another car horn blasted, and a late-model, jacked-up Bronco slowly came to a stop. The windows were rolled up, but when the door opened, a tall man with black hair hanging to the side in front of his face got out. His bright green eyes were chock full of fury. The crowd went eerily silent.

"What the actual fuck are you all doing on my lawn?" Dark Kane barked out.

"Interviewing for the crew," one of the men answered. "The announcement said today."

"Announcement?" a blond woman said as she

stepped out of the passenger's side of the Bronco. Her eyes were bright gold, and she made the air feel too heavy, right along with her mate. Winter had no doubt this curvy beauty was none other than the infamous Rowan Barnett, formerly of the notoriously violent Gray Backs, now the queen of these mountains and Second in Kane's Blackwing Crew.

"Air Ryder Croy—"

Kane held up his hand to cut off the man. "Stop right there, say no more." He slid a furious glance to the redhead sitting on his front porch in a rocking chair with his work boot up on the railing as though he didn't have a care in the world.

"Hi, fourth best friend." Air Ryder wiggled his fingers in a wave.

Under his breath, Kane murmured, "I'm gonna kill you."

Winter believed it. Kane's face was twisted into a feral expression that terrified her. A low rumbling noise filled the clearing. "Crew's full. Now get off my property."

"What? Hell no, I traveled all the way from Nevada to get in this crew!" one of the men yelled.

The mob went wild, yelling, questioning, surging

toward him, but despite Kane's deep limp, he wasn't backing down. He strode right up to the first shifter and closed-fist blasted him across the jaw. While the man went down like a sack of rocks, Kane caught the fist of the next one, then head-butted him hard. The sound of the man's nose breaking was audible even over the roar of the angry masses. Rowan leaned on the hood of the Bronco. She looked bored as she slurped on a red sucker and watched her mate level the rampaging idiots one-by-one. Ryder was on the front porch with a shit-eating grin stretching his freckled face. Winter would've laughed if an all-out riot wasn't happening in front of her very eyes. And also if she hadn't wasted her time driving all the way out here and getting her hopes up on a crew that wasn't even recruiting right now. They'd all been obviously duped by Air Ryder.

Logan stood.

"Where are you going, boy scout?" Dustin asked. "Don't you hear Kane breaking their bones? That dragon will kill you and laugh at your corpse."

Logan shook his head, and ignoring Dustin's warning, pushed his way through the fight. Winter stood on the log, balancing on her tiptoes to see what

Logan was doing. Dustin had been wrong. He wasn't going after the dragon at all, but he was pulling the mob back one by one, yelling at them, making space for Dark Kane to fight. And then Beast was there too, pushing the masses back with Logan.

"Fuck," Dustin muttered as he made his way toward them. "Move!" he yelled at someone who was standing in the way. When Dustin snapped his teeth at them and growled, the gooseflesh rose on Winter's arms.

"I'm out of here," the goth girl murmured. She strode off for the gravel road, but Winter stood there stuck. Did she get in the middle of a dominant male fight? Or did she make like Goth Girl and get the hell out of here?

Emma was standing on her log, too, neck craned as she watched the fight. If the human was brave enough to stay and see this thing through, then so could Winter. If for nothing else than to make sure the fight didn't migrate this way and hurt the frail girl. Winter wasn't as dominant as the brawlers, but she was a fast Changer, and her animal could fight well enough to protect Emma. She could at least buy her time to run.

The man who bumped her shoulder earlier Changed into a big, blond-furred grizzly and charged Kane. Two echoing clicks sounded and then fire, the shape and size of a soccer ball, struck the ground in front of the bear, stopping him in his tracks. And now Rowan, the fire-spewer, looked good and pissed. She jammed her finger at the grizzly. "You want to die today, you keep it up. You want to get into a Change-off in dragon territory, really? I'll fucking eat you. Leave."

The fire had brought the fight to a stop, and now the clearing was heavy with shocked silence and the scent of smoke and blood. Winter wondered how many noses Dark Kane had broken today.

The dark dragon himself stood close to the cabin, shoulders heaving, face like a beast, skin on his bulging arms cracking like concrete and cinching back together, cracking then cinching with every breath. And now Winter could see why Rowan had lost it. Dark Kane didn't have the best control, and mass Changes would summon his hellish monster from him. Rowan had probably saved everyone in this clearing, and they didn't even realize it.

Logan was standing closest to Kane, Beast next

to him, then Dustin, glaring down the crowd. This is what happened with hordes of dominant shifters. One mistake could trigger an avalanche of violence.

Kane snarled and spun, limped up the porch stairs, and disappeared inside, slamming the door behind him hard enough to rattle the tiny cabin. For reasons unknown to her, Logan slid a lingering glance to her. His eyes were bright silver, and crimson streamed from his lip. The neck of his T-shirt had been ripped, and there was a seeping gash on his neck. He didn't look in pain, though. He looked…concerned. *You okay?* he mouthed.

Winter checked behind her, but she was alone. Was *she* okay? She wasn't the one bleeding all over the dark dragon's front lawn. Jerkily, she nodded and mouthed, *You?*

Logan ripped his gaze away and spat red in the grass. Okay then.

Rowan disappeared inside, but Air Ryder was still leaning against the railing looking flushed. About half of the crowd was already drifting back to their cars, but to the rest who lingered, he said, "Fill out your applications, and I'll be back out with you shortly."

"So the crew recruitment is still on?" Dustin asked.

Air Ryder shrugged coyly. "Maybe." Then frowned down at his phone. "Is there a Winter Donovan here?" His attention went right to her, and his ruddy eyebrows arched high. "Winter of Red Havoc?"

Winter swallowed hard under all the attention that had suddenly been cast her way.

"No," she said, lifting her chin higher. "I'm Winter of Nowhere."

Air Ryder's lips stretched into a slow smile. "Good. Come with me."

THREE

What was happening? Winter's legs were numb as she stumbled off the log and made her way toward the lair of the dark dragon. It wasn't the cliff mansion she'd imagined. It was just a small cabin, and she was about to shove herself in that tiny space with two mother-freakin' dragons? And Air Ryder, who was one of the most battle-proven flight shifters in the entire universe. Oh, he might joke and look relaxed, but his eyes were blazing gold, and the closer she got to him, the heavier he felt.

Logan stood tall in front of her, head cocked as if confused by her, but he stepped out of the way as she approached. The clearing was silent, as though everyone was waiting for her to make her way to a guillotine or something. On a whim, she stopped at Logan and parted her lips to say something, but what? Her brain was on shut-down mode. Save me if I call? Come in there with me? He had no reason to do her any favors. She was a stranger. Something deep inside of her, some tiny instinct, told her she should fear this man, but she could also trust him.

When she looked up into his eyes, they were churning like silver storm clouds, and his teeth were gritted. He smelled of blood, and her animal reacted. Winter hissed at him before carrying on to follow Air Ryder up the porch steps.

Her cheeks heated with mortification. She'd hissed at a monster and then given him her back? Her instincts were broken. At the door, she cast a quick glance over her shoulder at Logan, but where she expected fury etched in his features, she found calculation and curiosity instead.

With a steadying breath, she stepped inside and closed the door behind her. Ryder was already making his way toward a hallway door where Winter could hear crashing and stomping from inside.

Ryder flung it open with an expectant smile and said, "Honey, I'm hooome," and then neatly ducked as a glass of water shattered against the wall behind him. "You wait here," he said, pointing Winter to a spot near the door.

"That close?"

Air Ryder ignored her and disappeared inside the room with Dark Kane. Brave snowy owl. Winter wanted to survive, so she stayed right where she was, near the exit and nearest Logan because she'd somehow convinced herself if she needed protection from dragon's fire, he was the monster to see.

Her inner panther nodded in agreement.

Ready to bolt at any moment, she sat on the very edge of a leather couch, hands clenched in her lap.

Movement caught her attention in the small kitchen, and Winter jumped as Rowan appeared. She filled a glass of water and leaned back on the counter, lips quirked up in a half-smile. "Rowan," she introduced herself.

"Winter."

"Of Nowhere, I heard. Are you one of Ben's panthers?"

"You know Ben?"

"I met him once. Kane knows him better."

"What the fuck, man?" Kane yelled in a muffled

voice through the wall. "You've done some dumb shit since I've known you, Ryder, but this is next level messed-up. I don't want a crew."

"But you have a crew, registered and everything," Ryder argued.

"I have Rowan. She's all I need. I'm not cut out to be a real alpha, or have you lost sight of that completely? God Ryder, have you seen me Changed lately? I don't have perfect control, not outside of Damon's facility, and now I'm supposed to build a crew under me? To protect? Fuck! You way overstepped on this one, man."

"You're freaking out—"

"Damn straight I'm freaking out! I've lived my whole life in the shadows. My whole life, and now I'm trying to build a friendship with the Bloodrunners, trying to be a good mate for Rowan, and trying to be a normal, decent—fuck! I'm the End of Days, Ryder. I don't need a crew under me. I need as little stress on my dragon as possible. I don't even like people!"

"You like me!"

"You forced me to! You with your surprise moonshine visits and fourth-best-friend talk, and...and...matching keychains, and Beer Fridays, and invites, and social media pictures, and hashtag-bro-dates, and aaaaaaaah!"

When Kane's yell tuned into a roar, Winter whimpered and hunched into herself. Rowan nodded and put her hand out in a comforting gesture that said everything was all right, but everything did *not* feel all right. The air was nearly un-breathable, and the house was vibrating with a power she'd never felt before. Discreetly, Winter leaned forward and pressed her palm onto the cool wood floors. The house was actually vibrating from Kane's rage.

"Winter of Nowhere, come in here," Ryder called.

"Who?" Kane asked in a gravelly demon voice. "And who the fuck are you calling?"

"Winter! I need you!"

Hell no, she didn't want to go in there. Kane was rattling the house, and she'd seen his dragon on TV. Fire breathing beast that looked like he was from Hell itself, nope!

"It's ringing," Ryder said. "Winter move them legs, woman!"

"Oh, my gosh," she murmured as she forced her feet to move in the direction of the office. "I'll be okay, right?" Winter asked Rowan as she passed, desperate for her terror to be put at ease.

Rowan shrugged. "Probably."

"What?" she whisper-screamed. But then Ryder appeared out of the open doorway and dragged her inside as Ben's voice came over the speaker of his phone. "Hello?"

Winter couldn't take her eyes of Kane's enraged face. She was gonna die today, right here in the lair of the dark dragon. She pressed herself against the wall as flat as she could make herself, and for the first time in her life wished her tits were smaller.

"This is Ryder. And Winter. And"—Ryder gave Kane a significant look—"Dark Kane. Kane, you remember Ben."

Kane's face went completely slack as he took a step back as though he'd been hit. "Ben?" he asked.

Ryder had the phone on speaker and was holding it out in front of him. Slowly, Kane approached, limping only slightly now. "Is it really you?"

"Yeah, man. It's me." Ben sounded tired, defeated even. "It's been a long time."

"I looked for you after…after…"

"I know. I didn't want to be found."

Kane exhaled a shaky breath and ran his hands through his dark hair, smoothing the longer tresses on top away from his face.

"You'll fight being alpha," Ben said low. "I know you will, but it's something you need that you don't realize you need. I was the same way and wanted to push everyone away after I lost my animal, but when I got him back, he needed something to stay good for. Do you understand?"

"I have Rowan. I have the Bloodrunners."

"You'll watch Rowan wither without a crew, and it'll make the dragon unmanageable. She's a Gray Back, man."

"No, she's a Blackwing," Kane gritted out, locking his arms on the desk and staring at a cork board of pinned, scribbled notes.

"But she was raised in Damon's Mountains around other people. Around other shifters. And even if she could deal with the loneliness, you can't. Your dragon needs anchors, Kane. He needs reasons to not burn the world to the ground when shit gets hard, and it *will* get hard. No more hiding, you're out there now. A problem shifter with black marks on your permanent record, in the news, in the media, speculated heavily about. You didn't want fame, I get that, but that little public dragon battle has landed you right at the top of everyone's attention. Not only does a crew need you for protection, but if you and Rowan get to breeding, you'll need them, too. Do you understand what I'm telling you?"

"Yes." Kane's voice broke on the word. He stood up straight and linked his hands behind his head. "Is Winter yours?"

"I'm hoping she'll be a Blackwing if you find she fits. She's good. A loyal one, but unpledged to any crew. This is me vouching for her."

"You calling in a favor?" Kane asked.

"Nah, brother. It's me who owes you. You were there for me when my brother died. You were there for me all those months in Apex. Winter is a gift. Not me begging a favor."

Kane narrowed his eyes at Winter and let off an explosive sigh. "*If* I decide to add to my crew, I'll consider her."

Ben murmured, "It's good to hear your voice again, Kane. Good to know you're okay after…well…everything."

Kane's frown deepened. "You too, Ben."

Ryder was smiling at Kane with the mushiest expression in existence when he ended the call.

"Shut up, man," Kane muttered as he strode past them both and exited the room. "We're still not okay."

Ryder dragged Winter out of the room with him, following on the heels of the dragon.

Kane paced in front of the kitchen. "Roe, what do I do?"

"Make the decision to add to our crew or not. As Second and as your mate, I'll back your play."

"What do you want?" he asked, approaching her. He placed his hands on her hips and rested his forehead on hers in such an intimate moment, Winter's cheeks heated with a blush. "Roe, do you need a crew?"

Rowan clutched his shirt and kissed him gently. "I need whatever makes you happiest."

Kane sighed and eased back, leaned his shoulders against the refrigerator and rocked his head back until he was staring at the rafters of the ceiling. "Winter will be my first interview, but this doesn't mean I'm adding to the crew—and stop clapping, you asshole," he griped at Ryder, who was in fact performing a victory slow-clap. "We'll see how

I feel about this after all the interviews are done. If my instinct is to keep my crew how it is, just me and Roe, then that's what'll happen. And no pressure from you," he barked out, jamming a finger at Ryder as he passed. "Roe, Second or not, you have just as much say as me." Kane threw open the front door and strode out onto the porch. "Listen up!" he yelled over the chaos and noise. "I will be taking interviews for my Blackwing Crew, but my decisions will be slow or none-at-all. It could take months for the final applicants to be fully considered, so if you're in this for the quick pledge, fuck off."

A few muttering shifters in the back spun and made their way back up the road.

Kane didn't seem to care at all because he continued. "Also, my territory is small, just a few mountains, so if I accept a crew, it will also be small. And I'm not going to be floating you. While you are going through the interview process, you will find your own job and lodging—"

"That's not how a crew works!" one of the shifters called out.

"It's how my crew works." Kane pointed to the gravel road. "If you don't like it, I trust you're smart enough to remember where you parked your car." He slammed his hands down onto the railing and locked his arms against it. "Moving on! *If* you get through this grueling interview process, and *if* I decide to pick up a couple members, and *if* you make the final cut, I still won't be floating you. There's a level stretch of land up the road I will make available for trailers, built to my specifications, which *you* will be paying for. And if you ever decide to leave my crew for any reason, you will forfeit said trailer, no matter how much of an investment you put into it. Is that understood?"

"Fuck this," another muttered, and several more turned and left.

None of this scared Winter off, though. It all sounded fair, and she liked the way Kane said it like it was. He reminded her of Ben, just way more terrifying.

Winter stood in the doorway, stunned to be on this side of the speech, eyes trolling for Logan, hoping he wasn't one of the leavers. He wasn't. He stood front and center, arms crossed, lips pursed thoughtfully as he nodded his head as though he thought the same thing she did. Sounded reasonable enough.

And for the first time in months, she looked forward to something. She looked forward to the challenge that lay ahead. From the small amount she'd seen of Kane, he wasn't an easy man to befriend. He would pick the best of the best here, the cream of the crop, the best combination of shifters that would mesh with his crew, and she suddenly hoped she would be one of them.

And she hoped Logan would be, too.

She would never admit it out loud, but Logan and Kane had just given her the most beautiful distraction from the shit-storm happening with Brody back in Red Havoc.

FOUR

When fifteen remained, Logan couldn't help but think Air Ryder's antics were either really stupid, or he was a secret genius. By not telling Kane he had advertised for a Blackwing Crew, the crowd had been witness to his violent reaction.

Kane had weeded out half the applicants by smashing faces and daring them to stay in his territory. And that shifter didn't make idle threats either. Logan had met few who he hated turning his back on during a fight, but Dark Kane was certainly one of them. He'd opened himself up to a fist to the face and this split lip in an effort to keep Kane in his peripheral. And he was fighting with him, not against him.

Yep, Kane was just what he needed. He wouldn't pussy out when it came time to put Logan where he belonged. Not like his last alpha. Fucker still made him mad for not following through. Any last shred of respect had been stamped out like a tiny sidewalk weed when Trey had refused to put Logan down. So here he was, trying to hold onto his steady long enough to make it into the Blackwing Crew so Kane would have a reason to give him an honorable end. So he could go with dignity.

Fuck, Winter was cute. All destroyed-looking like a little lost kitten who'd been through a pit bull fight and survived. Logan was having trouble paying attention to Dark Kane's speech because she was standing in the doorway, her eyes glowing gold like the fucking sexy big-cat she had tucked away inside of her. He hoped she was a panther, but she would make one helluva lioness, too. That little hiss she'd given him was about the sexiest thing he'd ever heard. Her hair, nipple-length and unbrushed with a few blond highlights grown out by inches, was straight down her shoulders. She was maybe six inches shorter than him, fit but curvy with those big titties that would feel perfect cupped in his hands.

Logan clenched his teeth. He shouldn't be thinking of her like this. She was a person, and from the ghosts in her eyes, she was going through hell right now. And why else would she be here? Two black-marked dragons heading up a crew? They would only attract the broken. That much was clear from the scent of sickness he smelled on the remaining shifters. No one was going to put up with this much effort to pledge to a crew if they weren't desperate.

Hell, that's why he was here.

Winter's eyes were on him again. Gold as the sun and surrounded by dark lashes, and she had a tiny, slightly crooked nose that said she snarled up one side of her lip too much. She looked tough. A green fitted T-shirt over black skinny jeans all ripped to hell, and black combat boots on her feet with the shoelaces undone. Her outfit was at total odds with the big-ass fancy purse she carried.

Logan canted his head and dragged his attention to those perfect tits she had stuffed into a push-up bra. He was usually really good at assessing someone in a glance. That's what he'd been trained to do. Winter, however, was an unreadable enigma.

"You got fuck-me eyes, Bear," Dustin said from beside him. He shoved Logan in the shoulder.

Kill him.

Logan took a careful step away from Dustin. Fuckin' werewolf was going to rile the monster and end his own life with one more of those stupid touches of his. Wolves were too damn feely for his animal's taste. If it was up to his inner bear, Logan would eat the entirety of the werewolf race and make the world a better place, but here in the dark dragon's territory, he had to play nice. Eating the competition would probably be frowned upon by Dark Kane and his sweet mate.

Logan almost snorted. He'd just thought of a dragon shifter as sweet? She'd just blown fire at one of the idiots who charged her mate. She was no pushover, but Logan could just about taste the sweetness wafting from her.

Winter wasn't so sweet. He bet she could tear him up in the bedroom. He would've let her, too, if his bear was okay to sleep with a woman. He wasn't, though, so Logan was stuck in hell as the eternal masturbator. God, he needed Kane to kill him quickly. Beast smelled sickest of all. He was too damn close and set Logan's bear on edge. That, and Kane gestured Winter back into the house and out of Logan's sight. Something about that made him want to pull the same shit that bear had and charge the Blackwing alpha. Kane smelled sick, too. This crew was fucked.

Kill him.

Who? Who the fuck was his bear even telling him to kill now? Just another psychotic day in the life of Logan Furrow.

He missed Winter. Missed staring at her. Missed the push-up bra. Missed smelling her. How long were these interviews supposed to last?

"Dude, stop it," Dustin said from where he was pissing beside the house. He gave him a narrow-eyed glance over his shoulder as he jiggled piss droplets from his dick. "Cool it with the growling. No one is even standing near you."

Was he growling? Shit. Beast was staring, his fists clenched and his nose all scrunched up as though he was half shifted already. Logan crossed his arms even tighter over his chest and swallowed the snarl.

Dustin was zipping up his pants now.

"You know there are cameras, right?" Logan pointed to one in the tree and one on the porch.

Dustin shrugged like it made no matter to him. "What'll Dark Kane see? Me marking my territory, big fuckin' deal."

Logan huffed a breath at his stupidity. "Well, good luck not getting eaten," he muttered as the werewolf passed him by and picked up a discarded application.

"Oh, he won't eat me. I'm a shoo-in for his crew."

"Why?" Beast grunted.

"Because," Dustin said nonchalantly. "I have something the dragon wants." And with that, he loped over to the log seats again and began filling out his application.

Moron couldn't have anything Kane wanted. No one did but his mate, Rowan. Anyone with eyes or senses could tell that Kane was a broken but simple man with simple needs. Rowan likely met every one of them, or he wouldn't be so pissed at having to do interviews in the first place. A crew needed Kane, but he didn't need a crew.

He'd liked the way Winter hadn't been able to take her gaze away from him. Liked the way her pupils got all small when she stared. Liked how she made him want to…want to…

Logan frowned. She made him want to do something he hadn't wanted to do in a long time. Protect someone. Protect her and, in a way, protect that mousy human, Emma, because Winter had been standing protectively in front of her during the fight, like the girl meant something to her. Like she would've been hurt if Emma had ended up in the fray.

He should've been paying attention and keeping the idiot mob away from Dark Kane, but time after time, he'd looked over at Winter to make sure she was out of the way and safe.

Stupid. She could take care of herself. She was a panther. Or a lion. Either way, she didn't need some broken man to be her make-shift hero. And besides, he was too damn dark to be anyone's hero. He was a nightmare instead.

"What's taking so long?" he murmured to Beast, who was mirroring his posture, staring at the front door ten yards away from them.

Beast grunted like a caveman.

"Dude," Dustin called. "They've been in there for ten seconds. Don't get in too big a rush to get rejected."

Logan wanted to kick Dustin's teeth in.

He picked up one of the fluttering applications blowing along the ground, but the front door opened up and Winter stood there, wide-eyed. Was she frightened?

Kill him.

"Rejected already?" Dustin asked.

"No," she said in that pretty bell-tone that said she could probably carry a tune. "Kane told me to stick around for group interviews. Logan, you're up."

He'd watched her lips form his name, and as she walked up to him, he had this overwhelming urge to kiss her quick so he could taste the lingering word on her lips. He stood frozen as she did something he hadn't expected in a million years. She gripped his shirt in a clenched fist and bumped her shoulder against his chest, rubbed her arm from one side of his ribcage to the other like he wasn't some terrifying animal. "Affectionate kitty," he whispered mindlessly. She'd made him drunk on her closeness. He wanted to fuck her in the woods.

Logan closed his eyes and held his breath until she released him, and when he opened them again, she looked just as confused as he felt. That, and she was standing ten feet away from him still on the porch.

She hadn't touched him at all. He'd just imagined it.

Kill him.

"Shut the fuck up," he gritted out to his bear.

Winter looked hurt.

"Not you!" He flung the application like a Frisbee and flinched his gaze away from the pain in her eyes.

"Smooth move, Romeo," Dustin called as Logan brushed past her to the door.

He should turn around and apologize to her, but what good would that do? It was just a selfish ploy to get her to see him as something he wasn't. For her to see him as decent. Best she figure out what he was now and stay the hell away. He wanted her to survive him.

In a rush, he shut the door behind him. Kane sat at a table, elbows on the polished surface, hands clasped in front of his mouth as he studied Logan. "Name."

"Logan Furrow," he answered, lifting his chin high.

Kane glared at him a few seconds too long, then pulled an open laptop closer and typed onto the keyboard, which gave Logan a few seconds to assess the situation. This part he was good at. That instant where he could take everything in and remember it for the rest of his life. The new-home sawdust smell that said Kane and Rowan had been renovating their lair, the dust motes that said he hadn't dusted in a week. The flipped corner of a rug near the back door that said someone had left the back way in a hurry. The buzz of a new refrigerator, marks on the beams of the ceiling that said the roof was new. The soft flutter of papers that said Kane probably had notes pinned to a wall somewhere. An office maybe. Down the hallway to the right. The frown on Rowan's face as she stood in the kitchen leaning on the counter. Not a threat. She smelled worried. Not offensive. Everyone felt uneasy when they got into tight spaces with him. Air Ryder's scent lingered, but he wasn't here anymore. He was probably the one who flipped the corner of the rug. There were three escapes. Front door, back door, and the picture window in the living room. A knife block sat on the counter, a fireplace set had a metal poker in it near the hearth, and that was all if he was too lazy to reach the six-inch-long Bowie knife he kept in a sheath at his ankle.

"Former Ten Rivers Crew?" Kane asked, arching his black eyebrow. "Why did you leave?"

"The alpha didn't cut it."

Kane's monstrous green dragon eyes narrowed. He leaned back in his chair, crossing his arms as he studied Logan. "In what way?"

Logan growled. "Because he broke a promise."

"Just one promise?"

Logan nodded his chin once.

"Must've been a big one."

"It was the only one that mattered to me."

Kane slid his computer out of the way and leaned forward on his elbows. "Logan Furrow. Your name sounds familiar. What did you do for work?"

Logan huffed a humorless breath. "Pass."

"Then you can leave."

Well, now he was directly in between a rock and a hard place. He would have to leave anyway if he admitted his career. "Any other question to start. Get to know me before you cut me out."

"Fine, what did you do to your bear to break him?"

That was basically the same question. "Nothing. He's fine."

"Liar. I can feel how fucked up he is all the way from over here. From the way my mate is bristling behind me, I'm guessing she can, too. So please illuminate me, Mr. Furrow. Why should I allow you to be in my crew?"

"Because I'm loyal, and I can protect you and your mate. I can protect your entire crew if it came down to it. I have a skillset."

"From your career?"

"Yes, sir."

"Name your job, Logan. I'm not going to ask you again."

"Mercenary. Assassin."

"Fuck," Kane spat out. He wouldn't look at him now, was shaking his head back and forth. "Your choice?"

Logan hesitated.

"Answer me."

"Not at first. At seventeen, I was ordered by my alpha to put down a problem shifter he couldn't muster the balls to put down. My bear was…" Logan inhaled deeply and spilled the rest of his sins in one breath. "He was dominant, and I was young, and I didn't know I could say no, and he hired me out after that."

"How many kills?" Kane asked low.

"Enough," Rowan said.

Kane made a tick sound behind his teeth and asked again, over his mate's wishes. "How many?"

That number was for Logan alone. It was his ticket to hell.

"Sit down," Rowan demanded, making her way to the table.

Kane shot her a warning look. "Rowan—"

"You said this was just as much my choice, and before we nix anyone, I want to know more than their career. I want to know them."

"He is his career."

Rowan cupped her mate's cheeks and smiled down on him like an angel. "You see things in black and white."

"I'm supposed to protect you."

"I'm a dragon, and I'm not his target." Rowan dragged her lightened eyes to Logan. They were gold now, with elongated pupils. "Sit down and tell me…what was the happiest day of your life?"

Shocked by her question, Logan stood frozen. This wasn't what he'd bargained for. He'd thought the interview would be to assess his capability of keeping the crew safe, not this personal shit.

Rowan arched her blond brows. "Sit."

There was dominance and order in her words, and he wanted to listen to her. He could practically smell the irritation on Kane, but he didn't want to disappoint the Second.

He missed Winter. He shouldn't be thinking about her right now, but he did. He missed the way she looked and smelled. He'd really liked the way he felt when he'd imagined her touching him.

If he didn't answer questions, Kane would send him away from here. Away from her.

His mouth was dry as a desert as he took the chair across from Kane slowly.

"Take your time," Rowan urged. "Think about it. Happiest day."

The chair creaked under him as he shifted his weight and angled his face, exposing his neck to the pair of subdued titans across the table.

Kill him.

Kane snorted and shook his head as if he'd heard

Logan's bear.

"Five years ago, almost to the day, I was sent to a crew up in the Appalachian Mountains. Cougars. Real backwoods, quiet. Big crew. They had a problem cat, alpha couldn't manage him anymore. He paid my alpha for my services with moonshine money. I was usually only brought in after the problem shifter had started killing, when their animals were out of control. This one was early. He hadn't killed yet, but he was close. He'd been stalking hikers, tempting himself. His alpha said he was obviously bloodthirsty, so it was a typical job, nothing out of the ordinary. I was supposed to go in and challenge him, let him go honorably, leave. It was going to be a one-day job."

"This is your happiest day?" Kane asked, looking disturbed.

"Just wait," Rowan murmured. "Continue."

"I got there, and I'd already grown this sixth sense about problem shifters. I could tell how far gone they were, and this one, Nick, wasn't far gone. He was salvageable. Hadn't got the taste of human blood yet, and so I stalled. I asked the alpha if I could take him out for a drink before the challenge. First time to ever do that. He agreed, thinking it was part of the gig, and I sat down in this old, shitty, hole-in-the-wall bar with the guy, and we talked. Really talked. I could tell he was trying, but the effort was new. And when I finally got him to fess up, he said there was a girl in his crew. She didn't give him the time of day because he wasn't right, but he'd been working harder in hopes he could get his cougar under control enough to ask her out." Logan chuckled at the memory and scratched his jaw. "It was the first time I refused a job. I told the alpha Nick needed more time, and that if he ended him, I was coming for the alpha. That I would put his entire crew under my fucked-up bear. So he had a choice. Boot Nick from his crew or put more effort into saving him."

Rowan smiled. "So your happiest day was when you didn't have to kill."

"Second happiest day." Logan pulled his wallet from his back pocket and plucked a picture of a sweet baby girl from behind his driver's license. He slid it across the table to Kane. "My happiest day was when Nick sent me this picture in the mail with a letter thanking me for giving him more time."

Eyes going misty, Rowan sat there with the picture held in front of her. Females did that—cried a lot. Kane sat stoically, eyes narrowed and thoughtful.

"You asked me how I fucked up my bear. I did that by killing when my bear didn't want to. I did it by not giving problem shifters enough time."

"Worst day," Kane said.

That was an easy one. "A month ago when my alpha went back on his word."

"Which was?"

Logan leaned back in the seat and met Kane's glowing green eyes. "To put me down. He'd promised me a set number of jobs, and then I was gonna have peace. He was dominant enough. One of the only ones in the world who could've bested me, but he liked that money too much, so he gave me another job instead."

Rowan set the picture on the table and turned her head away, but Logan could see it—the tears dripping from her chin.

"Did you do the job?" Kane asked in a careful tone.

"Nope. I left the crew. It was the first time I ever disobeyed him. I left my chance of dying the way I wanted." Logan leaned onto the table and dared a direct glance at Dark Kane. "Until you."

Kane stood and paced to the kitchen and back, running his hands through his hair, pushing it back from his face. "I'm not going to be the one to put you down, Logan. I'm really not. I'm struggling to control my dragon and killing won't keep me steady. It could put the world in danger. I'm not your solution."

"I'll do it," Rowan whispered.

"What?" Kane and Logan asked simultaneously.

The Second of the Blackwing Crew leveled Logan with a heartbroken look. "If you make it into this crew, and you get to a point where you need to be put down, I'll do it."

"Rowan, this is a bad—"

"You can join the others," she said, lifting her chin primly. "Send in that big fella with the scarred-up face next. Wait with Winter until we call for group interviews."

Logan sat there stunned, his palms on the table as he dragged his gaze from Rowan to Kane, then back again.

She'd just offered him hope. "Thank you," he murmured, exposing his neck. Jerkily he stood, and the chair behind him scraped across the floor. He made to leave, but remembered the picture and doubled back. He took it from Rowan's outstretched grasp and said it again with more feeling this time because death by dragon's fire was his last chance to end the hurt. "Thank you."

"Logan?" Rowan asked as he opened the door.

"Yeah?"

"I asked Winter who she thought would be good in this crew, just based on pure instinct, and do you know what she said?"

"No."

"She chose you. Maybe you aren't unsalvageable either."

Logan ducked his head to hide his deep frown. Rowan didn't know what she was talking about. If she spent a single minute in his deranged mind, she would Change into her dragon and end him now. But she'd just done him a favor by pushing him into the next round, so he didn't argue. Instead, he forced a smile and lied to make her feel better. "Maybe not."

FIVE

"Oh, my gosh," Winter whispered.

How did she wrap her head around all that Logan had just admitted to the dragons? She pushed off the house where she'd been eavesdropping near the back window and hurried around the corner. Fuck, oh fuck, oh fuck, Logan was a mercenary? And not only that, but he was on a mission to be put down? She wanted to cry, but he would see her tears and puffy eyes, and he would know what she'd done.

She bolted away from the house toward the trees. Once she was in the woods, Winter slowed her pace, acting like she'd just been taking a stroll through the forest.

"That was the longest piss in the history of

urine," Dustin called. "You pooped, didn't you?" He nodded and rolled his eyes. "It's okay, kitty, everybody poops."

Logan was standing by Dustin with his hands on his hips, staring thoughtfully in her direction. Mortification heated her cheeks. "I didn't poop, Dustin. I just took a walk."

"Somebody call the fire truck. Kitty's pants are on fire."

"Fuck you," she muttered.

"Fuck me?" Dustin asked, twitching his long hair out of his face. "Okay, is that on the table? You look a little small for my dick, but if we use tons of lube, you spread your legs wide enough, and relax your goody basket—"

"Stop it," Logan gritted out.

Power rippled through his words. Dustin let off a dog whimper and snapped his head to the side, exposing his neck. "Okay, okay, sorry," Dustin choked out.

Logan moved to the other side of the fire pit near Emma and sat down. Beast was nowhere to be seen, so he must've already been inside with the dragons.

Clenching her trembling hands to steady them,

Winter murmured, "I really wasn't pooping."

"Then what were you doing in the woods, hmm?" Dustin asked, rubbing his neck like it was sore.

With a shrug, she said, "Nothing."

Logan was staring at her clenched fists, though. "Were you eavesdropping?"

The direct question startled her. He would hear a lie, and now he was watching her so intently, there was no way she could wiggle out of this.

"Ooooh, curiosity is gonna kill the kitty," Dustin sang.

God, she hoped he didn't make it to group interviews.

Winter stalled by pulling her hair up into a high pony tail. "So, they still have to make it through all these interviews before they begin the group ones." She nodded her chin toward the fifteen milling shifters hanging in loose groups in the shade. "I'm starving. I think I saw a mom-and-pop burger joint down the road near the gas station. Anyone want anything?"

"Three hamburgers with everything on them, two orders of fries, and if they have milkshakes, I want chocolate, and also a strawberry one," Dustin said without missing a beat. "Extra-large like my—"

"Money," she interrupted, palm out.

"You aren't paying?"

"I would rather step into a legitimate bear trap than take a werewolf out to lunch."

"Rude," Dustin muttered, digging in his wallet.

"Emma?" Winter asked.

Apparently she'd turned her hearing aid back on because she nodded and told her she wanted a hamburger, hold the onions. When she reached for her purse, Winter shook her head. "On me," she said.

Emma watched her lips, so Winter made a mental note to enunciate things clearly when talking to her.

"That's not really fair, but okay," Dustin muttered as he slapped a twenty onto her palm. "I want change back."

Winter scoffed and shoved the bill into her back pocket. "You ordered all the food, Dustin. There won't be any change."

"Small towns cost less money," he called after her as she made her way toward the gravel road. "Aren't you going to wish me luck on my interview?"

"Knock 'em dead," she called with a wave over

her shoulder. "Tell more poop jokes. I'm sure they'll let you right in."

She'd avoided contact with Logan on purpose and would just get him the same thing Dustin ordered. She would even play super nice and order a meal for Beast, and maybe Kane and Rowan as well, even though she was a little miffed that Rowan had told Logan she'd recommended him for the crew. The interview stuff should've been private.

Hypocrite.

Dammit. Winter had eavesdropped, so she had no right to be mad at Rowan.

"I'll drive," Logan said from right beside her. Winter yelped and clutched her chest. How had he snuck up on her like that? He was huge, and bears had a tendency to lumber. Not him, though. He walked beside her with a smooth gait that didn't dislodge a single gravel pebble under his boots. Logan was scary. And sexy. But definitely scary first.

The thought of being trapped in a small space with him had her animal on edge, so Winter dragged her feet and looked back toward Kane's house. Toward the others, where it felt safer in large numbers.

Emma was cleaning up the discarded applications fluttering across the ground, and Dustin was watching the petit human with an unfathomable expression, his head cocked like a dog. Up on the porch, Beast was standing at the top step, so tall he easily gripped the edge of the roof in his hands and looked the epitome of a relaxed man. Except for his face. He was staring at Winter, warning in his eyes, and slowly shaking his head no.

Winter ran into a wall of muscle. Logan steadied her, strong grip on her upper arms. An ember of heat cracked between them, right where their skin met, and they both flinched away hard from each other.

"What did you do?" he demanded.

Her chest fluttered with the remnants of that shock. "I didn't do anything. M-maybe we should take different cars."

Logan had been stoic-faced since she'd met him, but for a moment, she swore she watched hurt flash across his face before it turned to stone again. "You're scared of me."

"I'm not."

"You are. I can smell it." He snarled up his face for an instant in an expression that was terrifying, but then it was gone, too, just like the hurt. "You're in no danger from me. Everyone else...maybe. But not you."

"That doesn't make me feel much better."

"You heard." He wouldn't meet her eyes anymore, and now he was leaning back against a white pick-up truck with black-out rims and huge mud tires. It was shiny and expensive looking.

"Does mercenary work pay well?" she asked, careful to keep the bitterness out of her voice.

Logan huffed a disgusted sound and stared off into the woods. And when at last he gave her his gaze again, his eyes churned light silver. "You stole from me."

"I'm no thief."

"You are. You listened in on something I didn't want to share. Absorbed it without my consent, and you didn't share anything back. Thief enough."

Winter narrowed her eyes and yanked the passenger side door of his truck open. "Get in," she growled.

Logan's lips turned up in a slightly wild smile as though he liked her sass.

The truck had that new car smell and was

pristine. The Silverado was detailed down to the cupholders with light gray interior, and even the floor mats were dirt-free. She clutched her purse in her lap like a shield as Logan gracefully climbed in behind the wheel. And as soon as he turned on the truck, before she could change her mind, she pulled the V-neck of her shirt to the side and closed her eyes tightly so she wouldn't see his reaction to the claiming mark on her shoulder. Her greatest shame.

She didn't have to see him to know his reaction. She could hear it in the snarl that rattled his chest and filled every molecule of air in the cab.

"You're claimed." It wasn't a question, and when Winter opened her eyes, he was gripping the steering wheel in a white-knuckled stranglehold.

"I thought I was. He chose another."

Logan frowned and released the wheel. "You didn't claim him back?"

"Oh, I did. I had it all. Perfect life. Perfect mate. Perfect future. He married my best friend two days ago. *Ex* best friend," she corrected. "They're going to have a little panther cub in a few months. Lynn will be covering the claiming mark I gave him with one of her own."

"You separated from your mate?" he asked, looking utterly baffled.

"No," she said, choking on the word. "He got Lynn pregnant while we were together. While I thought we were happy, he was breaking our bond and giving one to her."

"But that's not how it works. You don't just choose another. You claimed each other, so how the fuck did he even *see* another woman?" Logan shook his head and looked enraged. The air was too heavy to breathe comfortably, so she rolled down her window for some relief.

"You want me to kill him?" he asked in a low snarl.

"What? No!"

"Then why are you telling me this?"

"Because you said I stole from you and didn't give anything in return." Winter shrugged. "Now we both know each other's dark secrets."

Logan sat there, staring, silver eyes so bright they were hard to look at. Winter clutched her purse closer.

Logan sighed. "You're scary," he muttered as he looked behind him and backed out of a tight space between two cars.

Winter laughed—just one shocked sound before she asked, "Are you serious? I'm bottom-of-the-Red-Havoc-Crew submissive, can't even claim a mate right, and I'm about half your weight. You on the other hand…"

"I told you I'm not a danger to you."

"Hmm," she said noncommittally as he drove down the gravel road and away from the safety of the others.

Even if she wasn't one of his assassination targets, she hadn't been this excited and on-edge around a man…well…ever. That felt dangerous enough. And to top that off, he had no plans of sticking around. He was on a mission to get himself snuffed out of existence by a she-dragon. Just the thought of him dying like that unfurled poignant pain inside of her chest, and she barely knew him.

She shouldn't care. It was his life, his choice, but here she was, going weak over the someday-absence of a stranger.

Logan Furrow was the most terrifying man she'd ever met.

SIX

Logan finished paying for his food along with Beast's and the dragons'.

"Money-bags McGee," Winter muttered coyly, then took a sip of her to-go iced tea. "I guess you won't have trouble paying for your trailer if you get in the crew."

"Nope." He grabbed his ice water and pressed his fingers gently onto her lower back, leading her to a wall of stools that faced a long bench table in front of the window. The eatery was one of those hole-in-the-wall restaurants called Buff's Burgers. It was small, but tidy, and a couple groups of locals were laughing heartily on the other side of the room. Dark wood graced the floors, and black ink covered the white walls where people had written their names and drawn pictures all over it. Where she sat, there was a black marker, as though the owner encouraged the artwork. Huh. She liked this place.

"They're hiring," Logan said low as he pointed to the front window with a handwritten sign advertising such.

"You must have some mighty big confidence in my ability to get past group interviews if you're already looking at jobs for me."

He took the stool next to hers. "Why did they ask who you think would be good for the crew?"

Winter watched an old copper GMC truck coast by the front window. "No idea."

"They already trust your opinion to an extent. Well, until you threw my name into the ring. Rookie mistake. Don't pick the bad bet." He spun his Styrofoam cup in his hands with a faraway look. "Why did you say that?" he asked quieter.

"Why did I give them your name?"

"Yeah, that."

"Uuuuh." She sighed. There were a lot of reasons she wouldn't admit, and some of them had to do with how her nipples perked up like little tongue-seeking marbles around him. She could give him something, though. "You moved away from me when you figured out I was uncomfortable with your dominance."

"So."

"So, an asshole would've just sat there and made me uncomfortable. Dustin would've. And you offered to get us all applications so we wouldn't have to fight the fray. And you rushed to Kane's aid to make it a fair fight."

"That's not why I rushed to his aid. Too many shifters coming at Kane, and you know what he'd do? What he'd *have* to do because his animal is the fucking apocalypse?"

"End them all," she uttered on a breath.

"Exactly. I want to die, but not like that. Not with everyone screaming and running and Kane getting locked up in some shifter prison for mass murder."

"I don't like you saying that."

"What, about shifter prison? It exists."

"No, about wanting to die." Anger rippled through her. "Don't say that again. Not in front of me."

Logan's dark eyes tightened at the corners, but he nodded and muttered, "Fine. We'll pretend everything's okay."

"That's all I ask," she said sarcastically.

"Red Havoc Crew, huh?"

She gave a private smile at his attempt at small talk. She sucked at this stuff, too. "Six-hour drive away from here, up in the woods, mostly dudes except for me and the alpha's mate. And Lynn." She said the skank's name like curse.

"Was the alpha a good one?"

"Yeah," she said softly. "Ben was amazing when I came to him. I was a mess, and he cleaned me up."

"Yet, here you are."

"Here I am. Brody messed up everything. I can't stay in the crew and watch him build a life with Lynn and be okay, you know?"

"No. I don't." Logan poured a pile of salt onto the table and drew a question mark in it. "I've never had a mate."

"Ever get close?"

Logan snorted. "What female is going to settle down with a man like me?"

"You mean a murderer?"

Logan winced. "Yeah. That."

"I mean, women can be nuts. You just have to find one whose crazy matches yours."

"Easy as that, huh? Yeah, I never did that. There was a girl I liked once. She was human. Thought about trying to leave my crew, leave my alpha, and go straight, you know? Stop the jobs."

"What happened?"

Logan sipped long and hard on his water, then said, "She found out what I did for a living. Found out what I am." He gave Winter an empty smile. "Her crazy didn't match my crazy."

"Did you like the jobs?" she whispered. His answer meant so much.

Logan looked at her and, in just an instant, his eyes aged a hundred years right in front of her. "No."

"Then why did you do it?"

Logan leaned closer and closer until his lips were inches from hers. His eyes were troubled and locked on her mouth as if he would kiss her. She was terrified, but she was hopeful, and warmth pooled deep in her belly at how close he was. Logan brushed her hair back off her shoulder with a gentle caress, eased to her side, and then lowered his lips right beside her ear. He whispered, "Because no one else would."

"Your order is up," the man behind the counter

called.

Logan sat there for a moment longer, his lips brushing her earlobe, his cheek rasping against hers as Winter's heart pounded hard against her sternum, as if it was reaching for him. And when at last he disengaged, a mix of relief and disappointment swirled inside of her.

Logan picked the marker off the counter, pulled off the lid, scribbled his name on an empty patch of white on the wall, then dropped it and strode for the counter.

Stunned, she picked up the pen and wrote her name under his and, at the last moment, drew a heart between the two words, hoping he didn't look at her artwork before they left.

Looking like a wobbly fawn trailing a graceful stag, she stood on shaky legs and stumbled this way and that behind his easy stride. Logan grabbed the handles of the bags, doubled back, whooshed past her without a word, exited Buff's Burgers, and let the door close behind him before she could follow. Rude.

"Thanks a lot," she called after him as she trailed at a distance. When the scent of fur wafted to her on the breeze, she slowed, her alarm bells ringing.

"You shouldn't do that," he gritted out, shoving the food into the back seat of his truck.

"What did I do?"

"You shouldn't tempt me. You can't draw me to you, Winter. It isn't safe. Don't call my animal. And what the fuck is happening with your body. Are you in heat?" he asked from across the bed of his truck.

"What? No!" She didn't think so, at least.

"Well, you smell like you want sex, and trust me when I tell you, you don't want that shit with me. And I don't want it! Not from you." Logan got in the truck and slammed the door so hard the vehicle rocked.

Winter stood there in shock, opening and closing her mouth like a goldfish. But her anger snapped her right out of it. That, and cold iced tea hit her pants when she squeezed her cup too hard and pierced it with her finger. Mother fucker. She'd put the perfect amount of sugar and lemon in this one. It was basically a work of art. With a screech, she reared back to throw the leaky tea at his truck, but he yelled, "Don't you fuckin' do it!" in a muffled voice.

She was in it now, though, tits-deep in her fury so she threw it anyway, and it exploded against the glossy white paint with a satisfying splash.

The window rolled down slowly, and Logan was there, sunglasses over what were probably terrifying silver eyes. His muscles were rigid, mouth set in a furious little line. "Get in."

Hell no. She cared about survival. Winter flipped him off and marched toward the main road. Kane's territory wasn't that far, and she would rather walk across the damn Sahara Desert with bare feet than get into Logan's truck right now.

He coasted beside her, but she crossed her arms over her chest, lifted her chin primly, and ignored him.

His voice sounded defeated when he muttered, "It's ten miles to Kane's Mountains, woman. Just get in."

"Take it back."

"Fine, you aren't in heat."

She threw him a dirty look and walked faster.

Logan's sigh tapered into a yell that bordered on a roar. "Fuck, woman, what do you want me to say, and I'll say it?"

"I didn't ask you to sleep with me, Logan! You didn't have to say you don't want to have sex with me. I just told you I was epically rejected by my mate, and you throw your lack of physical attraction back at me? That's messed up."

"I'm not good at woman shit!"

"Noted, and I completely agree. Bye."

"I have a boner."

"What?" she asked, skidding to a stop on the asphalt.

Logan was leaning toward the passenger window, one arm draped over the steering wheel, jaw clenched. "I have a boner. From you. From wanting to..." He shook his head and stared out the front. "Please get in. I can't just leave you here to walk all that way."

Her phone dinged in her purse. Outside of Red Havoc, hardly anyone knew her number, so she fumbled to pull it out.

The message was from Brody.

I think I made a mistake. Where are you?

She read the text three times to make sure she wasn't imagining it. Hope and pain warred for her body. He'd finally figured it out? He'd made a mistake? Lynn was the mistake, not Winter? Her claiming mark burned. She had to get back to Red Havoc.

Wait, no.

Winter dropped the phone into her purse and gripped the straps closed to cut off her view of the glowing screen. Was she really that pathetic? Would she really go back to Red Havoc to pick up the scraps of Brody's leftover affection? Even if he wasn't happy with the pairing, he was going to have a cub with Lynn.

Winter would be the other woman now. No, this was just like him. He figured out she wasn't still pining for him and wanted to slither back into her heart so she could never really move on and be happy. She wanted to cry and scream and curse Brody's name. He'd ruined everything, and now he would make her the other woman? He would shame her even more. He would dissolve the final molecules of her remaining pride. For what? So he could have two females warring for his attention. That had been the game right?

Fighting a sob, she recklessly threw the door open and climbed in. "Take me away," she whispered, her breath hitching.

"Who was it?" Logan asked in a dead voice as he eased back onto the road.

Winter would rather gnaw off her arm than think about Brody anymore right now. It hurt too much.

"Was it him?" Logan asked louder.

To quiet him, Winter reached over and rested her open palm on his erection, then pressed down gently.

Logan tensed under her with a deep grunt. The steering wheel creaked under his hands. He let off a shallow breath and rolled his hips against her hand. That was all she needed.

He was long and thick, so hard under her touch, and she dragged her hand down the length of him. Logan swallowed hard, legs tensed, jaw clenched, soft growl in his throat that was so fucking sexy Winter got lost to it all.

She dragged her hand back up his dick and under the hem of his shirt until she could feel the warm skin of his rock-hard stomach.

"Fuck, fuck," Logan panted, chasing her touch with his hips.

He'd lied. He did want her just fine. She could tell

by how fast his control slipped with just a touch of her hand. Winter dragged her fingertips up the flexed mounds of his abs, then back down. She hooked her fingers right under the band of his jeans and pushed down until she brushed the swollen head of his cock.

Logan unbuttoned himself, then ripped his zipper downward before he grabbed the wheel with both hands again. And when Winter pushed his jeans and briefs down his hips, he lifted off the seat helpfully. God, he was beautiful. He had that muscular V, sculpted abs, and his dick was a perfect weapon against her defenses. Silken skin, throbbing under her touch already, cock so thick she could barely get her hand all the way around it.

The last wisps of Brody's betrayal vanished when she took the first long drag of Logan's shaft. The feral noise he made in his throat was so fucking sexy she couldn't stop now if she wanted. She had to finish this. Wanted to see his face as he came, wanted to hear his helpless noises, wanted to be the one who made someone lose their mind.

He rolled his hips with her strokes, pushing his dick into the tight hole she made with her fist, his body straining, breath uneven. At a barely-there turnoff, he yanked the truck off the main road and took a dirt track deep into the woods. He was so hard in her hand, so eager, she didn't expect what happened next. Logan slid his hand down the front of her jeans without warning, and the shock of his hand moving through her wetness was like a hit of a hard drug. She let off a long breath, spread her legs, leaned back, and gave him better access. Logan didn't play or tease. He went right for her core. He pushed a finger into her once, and on the second stroke, pushed in a second. Winter cried out.

The tires locked up and Logan skidded them to a rocking stop, threw the truck in park with his free hand, ripped off his sunglasses, and then his lips were on hers. It wasn't a gentle kiss, and there was no romance. This was two people who needed to escape their heads by getting lost in each other's bodies. His teeth scraped her bottom lip, and she repaid his roughness by biting his lip hard. He snarled and ripped at her pants until they were on the floor. She was whimpering now as she stroked his dick. He was getting close, and his pleasure was urging her own.

He was loud, groaning, cursing with each pull. His lips were everywhere—her mouth, her neck, her shoulder, her claiming mark. He nipped her hard, sucked enough to make bruises, and she fucking loved every second of this.

Winter arched back against the seat to give him a better angle to her neck and he pushed his finger into her again.

"Fuck, I'm gonna come," he gritted out. "Stop, stop, stop. I'm gonna come everywhere."

"That's okay," she whispered desperately.

"My clothes…I don't have anything else… Oh, God, Winter, I'm gonna come."

Winter released him and snarled possessively, clamped her teeth on his neck after he pulled her over the console and onto his lap. She eased up and locked eyes with him. He couldn't pass for human right now, but she didn't care. She needed him inside of her. Needed it like she needed air. Gripping his dick to steady him, she slid over him until he was buried deep inside of her.

"I'll catch it," she whispered against his lips and then rocked forward.

Logan slammed his head against the seat and rolled his eyes closed as if the pleasure was almost too much. Bright eyes, that snarl, the scent of fur…

She should be terrified, but she wasn't. She was purring louder with each roll of her hips and every bump of her clit.

Logan's hand was up her shirt now, under her bra, cupping her breast as he worked her neck and hugged her close. He matched her pace, rocking with her, gasping with her, groaning with her. Lost with her.

So close. "I'm gonna..."

"Come for me," he whispered against her neck. He pushed deeper into her, held her tighter, reared back and slammed into her again, faster. Their bodies made a slick sound together. She loved this.

"Logan!" she cried out as the first explosive pulse of orgasm rocked through her core.

He grunted in response as his dick throbbed inside of her, pouring warmth into her middle in jet after streaming jet. He ripped her shirt to the side, stretching the neck, and clamped his teeth over her claiming mark in a delicious tease. He groaned against her skin as he emptied himself.

Numb. Other than blinding pleasure, Winter felt nothing. She relaxed backward, allowed him to hold her as she let her hands go limp at her waist. With a drunken grin, she whispered, "That was amazing."

But Logan didn't respond, and his breath was coming faster, labored. The scent of fur was too thick, saturating every molecule of air. Winter opened her eyes, and what she saw dumped dread into her body.

Logan's eyes were blazing white, and his face looked feral. His muscles were twisting into something *other*, and the first echoing snap of bone sounded like a shotgun blast in the small space.

"Shit," she whispered.

"Run," he said in an inhuman growl.

But there was no running from the monster that was about to tear out of Logan. She hadn't even seen his animal, but she knew there was no surviving him. Frantically, she unbuckled Logan and shoved open his door.

"You said you wouldn't hurt me. You said. You said you wouldn't hurt me," she chanted over and over as she struggled to shove his heavy body out the door and onto the forest floor. He was trying to stay human, but he was losing to the animal. The building growl in his throat and snapping bones were proof of that.

"Go!" he roared, his face transforming into

something ferocious.

With a scream, she pulled the door closed, and threw the truck into reverse. In the middle of the quiet woods, a roar wrecked the silence, and a monstrous bear ripped out of Logan's skin. He was bigger than any furred shifter she'd ever laid eyes on. A true titan brown bear with teeth the size of a sabertooth, a back that was taller than the truck.

"Oh, my God," she whispered in horror as he stood to his full height in front of her and opened his mouth for another roar.

Winter jammed her foot on the gas and looked behind her to make sure she wouldn't crash into a tree. If she wrecked now, he would devour her just as surely as any man-eater dragon.

When she glanced in front of her again, Logan was right there, charging her, his eyes empty, his long, six-inch black claws sinking into the dirt with each sprinting step he took.

Terrified, Winter slammed on the brakes and threw it into drive, spinning the truck sideways. Logan hit her hard on the passenger's side, swinging her several yards and shattering the window. His long claw reached in and raked across her arm. She screamed at the pain as she stomped on the gas. The truck fishtailed, struggling under the bear's massive weight, but pulled free. Logan was right there on the edge of her blind spot, keeping up no matter how fast she sped up. He knocked his shoulder against the bed of the truck and sent her skidding sideways. No time to straighten out, she kept on the accelerator and sped through the woods, then pulled a wide circle until she could angle back to the road, all the while hearing the panting breath of the bear close through the broken window.

Winter was crying, nearly hysterical by the time she blasted onto the main road. Logan skidded to a stop in the middle of the paved street and roared loud enough to rattle her ear drums.

And as she watched him in the rear view disappear, she had an awful, gut-wrenching thought.

Rowan had been wrong.

Logan the man was perhaps salvageable.

His bear, however, was not.

SEVEN

The pain made it hard to think. Winter stumbled to the motel office. It was a ratty, run-down joint with maybe two dozen rooms all connected on one long L-shaped floor, but it would have to do until she could get the bleeding to stop.

"I need a room," she panted desperately to the man at the front desk.

"Good God, girl," the balding gentleman said, his eyes trained on the oozing slash marks on her arm. "Have you called an ambulance?"

"No, no ambulance. I'm a shifter. I just need an hour or two of rest. Please sir, I need a room." She was going to pass out soon if she didn't find a dark place to sit down.

He gave a worried look to the destroyed truck she'd parked sideways in front of the office. The window had jagged pieces of glass sticking out, and the bed was crushed inward over the back wheel that had been making a scraping sound the entire drive here.

"Car accident," she lied. "Off in the woods, no one else involved, but I need somewhere to rest. Do you take a credit card?" That way he wouldn't think she was on the run and turn her away.

"Yes, of course. Forty-five even. You can take the room on the end, ten-ten."

Winter frowned. That was the number she'd seen on Kane's cabin, too. Funny. Or it would've been if her arm didn't feel severed from her body right now. She struggled out her wallet and paid. And right before she walked out of the office, he tossed her a first-aid kit and wished her luck. "Thanks," she said, and meant it. Sometimes people freaked out when they found out she was a shifter, but he'd been nice. Helpful even.

One-handed, Winter drove the truck to the front of 1010 and stumbled inside.

The room smelled of mildew, but it was dark and

quiet, and it would do. Desperately, she ripped open the first-aid kit and downed the four pain pills that came stock, then made her way to the bathroom, stripped out of her clothes, and hit the warm tap.

She smelled like a crime scene, and the scent of copper was so thick it was riling up her already frightened animal. She couldn't add the pain of a Change, so right now she was in keep-the-skin mode.

She sobbed the second the water hit the claw marks that ran from her chest across her arm. She didn't want to look, but she needed to. Her healing was working, but the injuries were bone deep and would take a few hours to stop bleeding.

The bathroom filled with steam, and still she sat in the tub, heart feeling like it was just as shredded as her arm. All she'd wanted was to forget about Brody for a while, but now she would have these scars for always. Every time she looked in the mirror, she would remember today. Remember this time in her life.

She was missing the group interviews for this, but she couldn't go back to Kane's. Not right now. Not until she was strong again and wouldn't set off those other predator shifters. They would sense her injury, sense her weakness, and attack. It was instinct.

But that wasn't the biggest reason she was hiding in a hotel instead of participating in another interview. There was one much bigger reason that took up most of her headspace right now. She was protecting Logan. If Kane and Rowan saw how far gone he was, how easy it was for his bear to attack, they would put him down on the spot. She shouldn't care, but there was something about Logan. Some mighty strength that battled with a deep break in the make-up of his being that called to her protective instincts.

Even if he couldn't be saved, she didn't feel done with getting to know the human half of him.

The front door clicked and opened in the other room. Winter froze, terrified like a little field mouse with no cover. She could smell him—Logan.

With trembling fingers, she moved the shower curtain aside, and there he stood, looking as wrecked as she felt.

His hair was mussed, his skin pale as a phantom, and the clothes he wore didn't fit well, as if he'd stolen them off some line of laundry somewhere. It was his eyes that held her, though. They looked a hundred years old, and exhausted.

He dipped his gaze to her arm and grimaced. Hooking his hands on his hips, he stared at the floor, swallowed over and over. "I can't have intimacy. The bear… I don't know what to do with it anymore. But you smell so fucking good, you're so soft, and you make me forget things. I lost my head, and it got you hurt. I can't…" Logan ran his hands down the dark scruff on his face and heaved a sigh. "You smell scared again, and I hate it. Hate this. Hate the way I am. If I could go back and change everything, I would. I would be settled in a crew. An alpha maybe. Someone good. Someone people could look up to. I wouldn't be here begging an honorable death from people who don't know me and don't owe me anything. I wouldn't be here hurting your chances at a new beginning, and you…you wouldn't be crying because of me. Do you need me to leave?"

Winter couldn't even sense his bear anymore, as though he'd tucked the monster so deep inside of him, he barely existed. Just like when she'd first walked into the circle of shifters today, and he'd been invisible. She shouldn't, but she felt safe again. She slowly shook her head, inviting him to stay.

And then he did something that shocked her to her bones. He peeled off his shirt. She'd expected scars all over his body from the problem shifters he'd fought, but his skin was smooth and void of any damage. That was telling enough. Logan was very good at battle. Something about that made her so sad. She'd heard his admission. His alpha had forced him into that first mercenary job at the tender age of seventeen. Dominant brawlers like him wielded a huge instinct to protect. It's why the dominants made such good alphas. But instead of protecting, his alpha had hired him out to kill.

Logan's bear had never stood a chance.

He kicked out of his pants and stood up straight, locking eyes with her, daring her to look. His shoulders were more defined than she'd imagined. He had a tattoo of a cross on his ribs, and another abstract tattoo covered one pec and flowed up to his shoulder and down his arm in a full sleeve. He was cupping his dick, covering it as her eyes dragged down his chiseled chest and the hard mounds of his abs, but when she reached his hips, he pulled his hand away and strode toward her.

Logan stepped into the tub, slid in behind her,

hugged her tightly against his chest, and buried his face in her neck. Winter sat there frozen in disbelief that this giant, complicated man had just exposed himself physically and emotionally to her.

For a while, he didn't say a word, but this was his apology. She knew without a shadow of a doubt he didn't give affection freely, or perhaps ever.

"Why?" she asked thickly. "Why did he hurt me?"

"Because he's broken. I broke him. He was good, and I made him kill, and now I'm the one who needs the mercenary."

"Rowan is your mercenary?"

He nodded against her neck. "I want to go fighting, with honor, but you've seen me. Who can beat him?"

"Only dragons." No other shifter on earth was as big or dominant or bloodthirsty as Logan's bear.

Winter turned sideways in his arms to face the wall, curled her knees up and rested her head on his bare chest, stared at the lines of grout between the bathroom tiles. "I'm angry at you."

"You have every right to be."

"Not because you hurt me, Logan."

"Then why?"

"I'm angry because you didn't save him."

Logan dragged in a deep breath and stroked her wet hair. "I'm angry for the same reason."

****

Should he tell her why he'd marked her? Winter was soft and hurt. That asshole mate of hers had busted up her insides and made her hunch into herself, just a ball of cement against the world with hairline cracks that let her sweet demeanor leak through. She probably thought that was weakness, but it wasn't.

He couldn't tell her his bear wouldn't have killed her. That he was just trying to make sure she was scarred forever. The fucked-up monster in his middle had claimed his mate in only the way Logan's broken bear could. Without permission and too roughly. Too much pain, too much blood—that was Logan's punishment.

She'd checked her phone on the side of that road, gone pale from a message Logan just knew was from her ex-mate, and something awful had happened inside of him. The possessiveness had nearly blinded him, and that first touch of her hand on his dick had sealed her fate. It was clear as water what she was doing. She was using him to forget Brody. But Logan's bear would be good-goddamned if he was a balm for that prick.

He'd grown desperate to make her belong to only Logan. And when Logan had refused to give into the temptation to bite her right over Brody's claiming mark, his bear had revolted and forced the issue. He'd created chaos and trauma that Winter didn't deserve. Even now, his bear was constricted in his middle watching her, adoring her, stalking her like the fucking psychopath he was.

What was it? Was this some messed up way for his bear to try to save himself? By attaching to something beautiful. To something whole and perfect. Was this bond Logan felt in his chest some desperate attempt to chain himself to this world?

It wasn't fair to Winter. They were strangers, and it wasn't her fault her kindness had earned the devotion of a beast.

Look what he'd done to her in one day. She was naked in his arms, broken down sobbing, arm still running pink under the steaming shower water. This was his effect on people he tried to care for.

Logan hated himself for what he'd done. For

what he'd allowed. He hadn't been able to stop the bear from marking her, but then, he hadn't tried that hard, had he? He could've put up a bigger effort to stop the Change. He could've held on until she sped away. But he didn't. He lost himself in the stupid momentary idea that he could keep something beautiful like Winter, but he couldn't.

He was a hurricane, and she was a butterfly. A butterfly with an inner strength that showed in how she was handling the aftermath of his attack, but a fragile-winged butterfly nonetheless. What chance did she have against the storm that raged within him?

Winter was his mate, a desperation-claim after just a few hours of knowing her, but he could never, ever tell her that. Nothing had changed from this morning until now. Logan was still on a straight path to Hell, and she deserved better than another mate who would leave her alone in the world.

EIGHT

Logan was toweling off his dark hair in front of the mirror, but Winter didn't miss his anxiety. He tossed a narrow-eyed glare over his shoulder as her phone vibrated in her purse again. She'd been doing a damn fine job of ignoring it, but Logan's attention had her instincts riled up. With a sigh, she quickly pulled on the T-shirt Logan had brought her. Apparently, he was staying a few doors down and had his luggage already sitting in his room, which would explain how he had tracked her down so easily. There weren't many motels around here.

Mentally preparing herself, Winter sat on the edge of the bed and plucked her phone from her purse. One glance at the screen, though, and she frowned at all the missed calls—nine of them. None from Brody, all from Ben.

"It's the alpha from Red Havoc," she murmured in quick explanation as she connected a call to him.

"Where the fuck are you?" Ben asked on the first ring without a greeting.

"A motel. Why?"

"Kane called, asking if you quit the interview process already. He's almost done with group interviews. Please tell me you didn't already walk away."

"Brody texted me."

"Shhhit. Winter, don't come back here for him."

"I'm not! I'm just telling you what's happening with your crew. He's one day married and reaching out to me, Ben. The entire point of this was for me to move on, right?"

"I'll order him to leave you alone if you just stay and try for the Blackwing Crew."

Winter lifted the gray cotton sleeve of the T-shirt and studied the angry-looking claw marks across her arm. They were bright red and indented, but the bleeding had stopped, so there was that. "I'm headed to Kane's territory now."

"Great!" Ben said, sounding pissed. "Don't fuck this up."

The line went dead, and she tossed the cell into her purse and flipped it off. "We have to go. Group interviews are almost over." She tossed Logan the keys to his smashed-up truck and smiled. "You can drive."

Logan snorted and shook his head as he made his way across the room to the door. "I was mad about you throwing an ice tea on it." He threw it open and squinted into the sunlight. "Now look at her."

"Your truck is a *her*?" she asked, following him outside.

"Whoa, you sounded really judgmental right there."

"You keep it pristine. Women aren't like that. We're messy and complicated. Organized chaos." She yanked the truck door open, spilling glass from the shattered window as she did. "What did you name her?"

"Victoria."

Winter plucked glass pieces off the seat. "You have a big, badass, jacked-up truck and you named it Victoria."

"It's a sexy name." His voice was deep and low, but there was a tinge of amusement laced in it.

"Well, sexy Victoria now looks haggard."

He winced as he looked down the side of his truck, the one he'd kept so polished and perfect. "I deserve that."

She made to climb up into the cab, but stopped herself, turned on a whim, and hugged his waist. Logan froze under her embrace, one hand gripping the top of the open door, the other thrust out in the air, palm up, as if he didn't know how to hug her back. She thought he would soften over time, but he didn't. He remained rigid until she slipped her hands off his waist and took a step back.

Eyes downcast, he murmured, "You shouldn't do that anymore."

"But you just held me in the shower," she said, confused.

"That was the last time we'll be sharing anything like that. It would be best if we just forget today happened. I'm not yours."

"And I'm not yours," she huffed.

Logan's dark eyes narrowed, but he nodded once. "So we don't need to go all affectionate, Winter.

We aren't a crew, we aren't friends, we aren't anything." He strode around the front of the truck and got in behind the wheel, flashed her a fiery glare, and started the engine as if he would leave whether she got in or not.

"You aren't really like this," she said.

"Like what?"

"So hot and cold." Winter climbed in and closed the door beside her. It was all bent up, but it clicked into place with a little extra elbow grease.

Logan turned up the radio. Some song about love and pain being the same thing. Perfect.

"We aren't *nothing*, Logan. We aren't strangers anymore, not after everything we went through together today. Even if I don't meet your qualifications for a friend, there is a chance we could be in the same crew. You want to pretend like today didn't happen? Fine. Big fuckin' surprise you're just like everyone else. I liked being with you before you Changed. It felt good."

"It was a distraction."

"So? We fit! Our bodies were good at what we did. And you can't pretend I wasn't a distraction for you, too. You want to forget some casual fling in the woods, okay. I didn't expect anything complicated from you, Logan. Just...don't be mean."

"How many men have you been with?"

She huffed a breath and dipped her hand out the broken window, caught the wind in the bowl she made. "None of your business."

"Seven."

She tossed him a dirty look. "I didn't ask your number." And she sure didn't want to hear about it after the emotional roller coaster that was today.

There was blood on her jeans. She could smell it. Even if the soreness in her arm didn't remind her of what they'd shared earlier, the copper scent sure did. He'd loved her body, and then he'd scarred her. She winced and returned her gaze out the window as buildings gave way to thick Smoky Mountain forest.

"I wouldn't have killed you," he said, barely audible over the music.

"I trust you." Winter didn't even try to conceal the lie from her tone.

"I swear I wouldn't have."

Across her mind flashed the vision of that charging bear, glass shattering, the massive claw bigger than her face reaching for her, bleeding her.

Apparently Logan-the-man was crazy, too. She'd seen the feral determination in that animal's eyes.

"Two," she murmured just to change the subject. She rolled her head on the seat and looked at Logan's handsome profile. Beautiful face, ruined soul. "Brody was my first."

"I was your second?" he asked.

"Lucky me," she said, holding her finger and thumb up in front of the sun. Squinting, she squished it between her fingers.

"I liked being with you too. You know...before. You were good at fucking."

Winter snorted and giggled. "Thank you. I think that's the nicest thing you've ever said to me."

Logan chuckled a surprised sound, and there it was, that stunning smile she knew would transform his face. "Since I've said so much to you."

"You are a man of few words."

"I'm a man of action."

"Murder and fucking. I bet Kane and Rowan will be thrilled to induct you into the crew."

"I have a skill-set that can help them."

"Until you convince them to put you down."

The song switched to a slower beat. It was one of

those with violins and a woman's soulful voice.

"Logan?"

"Yeah?"

"If they ask you to Change, you should get out of it. Kane won't let you around his mate if he knows what you are."

His smile faded to nothing. "What I am," he repeated. "You know what I am, and you're still sitting in my truck with me."

"I'm different."

"How?"

"Kane has everything to lose." When Logan dragged his eyes off the road to her, she smiled sadly. "I'm Winter of Nowhere, remember? I have nothing to lose."

NINE

"About time," Dustin called as Logan reached the others with the bags of cold food.

He'd zoomed away from her as soon as he was able, without a single glance back to see if Winter was following. So it was going to be like that now. Fantastic.

"Are you okay?" Emma asked in that thick voice of hers. Her eyes were already big in size, but right now, they were *huge* as she stared at Winter's arm.

Shit, she hadn't covered the claw marks well enough. "I'm fine."

Emma arched her eyebrows high and looked at the smashed-up truck. And before Winter could stop her, the little hellion charged Logan and shoved him as hard as her flimsy human arms could manage. He barely moved, but he looked away, exposing his neck. On the second shove, he held up his hands in surrender.

"You hurt her," Emma blurted out, shoving him again.

"What's going on," Dustin asked, a suspicious glance to where Winter was tugging her T-shirt sleeve lower.

Behind Logan, who was still getting push-pummeled by the tiny honey-haired lady, Beast snarled and gripped the back of Logan's neck roughly, yanked him backward out of the way of Fists of Fury.

"You hurt her?" he snarled out in a terrifying voice. The scars on his face went red right along with his angry flush.

Pulling Emma away from Logan, Dustin told her to, "Cut it out."

She kneed him neatly and swiftly right in the ballsack.

"Oooow," Dustin howled, releasing Emma immediately and doubling over.

"Don't touch me," Emma said.

Beast and Logan were locked up now, scuffling, hands around each other's necks and snarling, so Winter rushed to separate them. Her fingers scrabbled desperately for purchase, but Beast and Logan as men were evenly matched. Beast didn't know what Logan hid on the inside, though.

"It was an accident!" she yelled. "Beast, stop!"

The air was getting so heavy she was suffocating.

"You stupid human, I was trying to help you," Dustin growled at Emma from where he lay on the ground cradling his dick. "Can you not feel him? You were shoving a monster! Fuck!"

Emma dropped down with a confused frown on her face and patted around Dustin's privates as though that would cure the dick-kick. Dustin swatted her away none too gently, but Emma was persistent, and the two warring titans in front of Winter were now coming to blows.

Beast slammed his fist against Logan's jaw, and Logan landed the same on Beast's face in a blur. Shit! Winter got yanked down with them as they fell into a heap of flying fists.

"Group D," Rowan called from the porch.

Winter froze, her arms wrapped around Beast's

massive bicep. The others froze, too.

"Or should I say D-Team," Rowan corrected, one eyebrow arched. "Please release each other's necks and balls and follow me."

There were about ten shifters in a loose group near the tree-line, and all of them were laughing, the asshats.

Dustin struggled to get up, still holding his crotch, and Beast and Logan shoved each other hard before they let go their death grips. When Winter was pushed backward with the force of the two disengaging, Logan snarled like a demon, eyes bright silver as he stood and launched at Beast again.

"Now!" Rowan yelled, power crackling through the air.

Emma was already to the Second of the Blackwing Crew. Dustin called her a "butt-kisser," before he stumbled on a pile of spilled, cold french fries and loped after them. He was all hunched over like Emma had kicked his balls up to his belly button. Winter had to stay at the slow pace the titans walked because they were still glaring at each other and needed someone to walk between them to keep them separated.

Kane stood in the doorway of the cabin, arms crossed over his chest, bright green dragon eyes narrowed on their rag-tag group.

As they entered the cabin, Kane barked out, "Over there." He jammed a finger at a couch that would only sit three and paced back and forth across the room as they took their seats.

Winter sat between Dustin and Emma, and the titans stood like pissed-off sentries on either side of the couch, eyes full of fury and locked on each other. The volume of their snarling was ridiculously high and drowning out everything so Winter barked out, "Logan, don't ruin this for me."

He dipped his silver gaze to her immediately, and she could see it—the slight dilation of his pupils that said part of him wasn't broken. Taking care of more submissive females was a base instinct for dominant males. With a deep, baffled frown, he gave his attention to the wall and stopped the awful snarling sound in his throat.

Both Beast and Logan were bleeding, Beast from his forehead and Logan from another split lip. The air smelled like pennies.

"Do I even want to know what happened out

there?" Kane asked.

"No," Winter, Logan, and Emma said at once, while Dustin muttered, "Probably," and Beast grunted like an animal.

This was ridiculous. There wasn't a worse matched group of people for a crew, yet they were all sitting here trying just the same. D-Team was exactly right.

Beside her, Emma laughed. Winter pursed her lips against a laugh and kept her gaze carefully on Kane. If Winter looked at Emma's smiling face right now, she would lose it in a fit of giggles.

Kane looked like he wanted to murder all of them. "You think this is funny?"

Winter dared a glance to the side where Dustin was fighting a grin while shaking his head no. "Not funny at all, sir."

"Why the fuck is everyone bleeding?" Kane asked loudly, his black eyebrows arched up high.

"Because they're junior Gray Backs," Rowan muttered from the kitchen where she was eating a purple popsicle.

"Who started it?" Kane asked.

Everyone looked straight at Logan except for

Winter. She was no rat.

Dustin spoke up in a bored tone. "Not that I care, but Winter came back with a big old bear claw mark down her arm. And she smells like pain. And sadness. And she owes me twenty bucks."

Kane smelled good and furious as he leveled Logan with that dragon glare of his. "Did you hurt her?"

Logan nodded his chin once.

"Get out," Kane spat.

Logan made to leave, but Winter stood in a rush and cut off his path to the doorway. "Wait, wait, it's not what you think."

Kane approached in a blur and ripped her sleeve upward. Winter winced as his fingertips brushed the sensitive skin.

"Don't touch her," Logan gritted out, rounding on the alpha.

When Beast, Logan, and Kane all surged into a pile of violence, Winter screamed, "He's mine!"

"What?" Logan said, his shirt in Kane's clenched fist.

"His bear had an accident. Part of that was my fault. He warned me. Stop!" she shouted, pushing

Beast back by the chest. He had about a hundred pounds of muscle and a foot of height on her. "If he leaves, I leave, too."

"Fine," Kane said. "Both of you get out."

"Veto," called Rowan. "What do you mean he's yours?"

"I mean..." Winter swallowed hard and looked around at all the expectant faces. "He's my friend, and he deserves a shot at the crew." Or at least a shot at going out how he wanted.

Kane released Logan's shirt and jammed his finger toward the wall where he'd stood earlier. Exposing his neck, Logan made his way slowly to the wall. Submissive he may look, but his eyes glowed, and the snarl in his throat was back. He was playing nice for a shot at the crew. Nothing more.

Kane strode to the door and yelled, "Call-backs are tomorrow. If you don't hear from me by ten in the morning, you aren't up for my crew. Goodnight!"

Kane slammed the door and dragged a chair noisily out from under the table. "I'm tired. I didn't want to do this shit in the first place, my dragon has been a pill to manage today, and I have zero patience to sift through whatever shit-storm got Winter that injury. I will say that scars like that will not be tolerated in my crew."

"Well..." Rowan said, slurping purple syrup off the popsicle stick. "I am not so bothered by that as long as it's not malicious."

"What?" Kane said, looking appalled.

Rowan shrugged. "The Gray Backs fought all the time. These idiots remind me of home in a big way. At least they were laughing afterward."

"I'm not laughing," Beast said.

"At least *most* of them were laughing," Rowan conceded. "Sometimes crews can be like that."

"Violent little heathens?" Kane asked too loud.

"Well, yeah. It worked for the crew I grew up in. Not saying this should be an all-the-time thing, but a little brawl here and there is okay."

Kane groaned and rubbed his hands down his face for too long to be polite. Maybe he had a headache.

"Biggest fear," Rowan called across the room. "Don't think too hard, just answer the questions as they come. Emma, you start."

"Biggest fear?" Emma glanced at Winter, but hell if she knew what the dragons were looking for. Emma hesitated only a second before she said, "Failing."

"Getting too attached," Beast gritted out.

"STDs," Dustin said easily, like shifters could even get those.

Logan pressed his back against the wall and slid down until he sat on the floor, his elbows resting on his bent knees. "My biggest fear is that no one will ever really know me." He looked over at Winter, and there was a charged moment between them.

"Same," she murmured.

"Ugh, just fuck already," Dustin complained. "Or wait, did you already do that?" When his eyes widened, a lightbulb practically went off over his head. "Is that where you got the claw marks? Kinky."

Heat blasted up Winter's neck and warmed her cheeks.

"Next question," Rowan rushed out, but she was looking at Winter with a spark of curiosity in her blue eyes. "Why did you leave your last crews?"

Emma shrugged and said, "Boredom."

"Don't pretend you had a crew," Dustin scoffed.

Emma smiled brightly and zipped her lips.

"Right?" Dustin asked, uncertainty tainting his voice as he looked around at the rest of them. He ran his fingers though his hair, smoothing it back from his face. "Because humans don't have crews. You mean your family...right?"

Kane and Rowan were smiling now as if they were in on the secret, and little Ms. Human Emma just got a whole lot more interesting.

"Maybe that's where she learned to drop a shifter," Logan said.

"Oh yeah, kicking a man in the dick is such a skill."

"It looked pretty skillful to me," Winter said. "I thought you werewolves were supposed to be fast."

Looking grumpy as hell, Dustin flipped her off and crossed his arms over his chest.

"No crew," Beast said.

"Boy problems," Winter admitted.

"Alpha was a lying asshole," Logan murmured.

"Why do you want to be part of the Blackwing Crew?" Rowan asked as Kane relaxed back into the chair and linked his hands behind his head, eyes on them and seeming to miss nothing.

"I like dragons," Emma answered.

"I also like dragons," Dustin said, but there was a false note in his voice.

There was something strange about the way Kane looked at Dustin. Every time his glance slid the werewolf's way, it hardened and filled with some deep, dark emotion that gave Winter chills. This look he gave Dustin was no different. "Try that one again."

Dustin growled, but he wasn't meeting Kane's eyes anymore. "I got sick of being bottom of my pack."

"So you'll be bottom of the crew here?" Winter asked. "Good decision."

"Screw you. Oh wait, Logan already did."

"Do you want to die?" Logan asked him blandly. His face was all twisted and full of murder though, so Dustin exposed his neck like a wise dog.

"I need an alpha more dominant than me," Beast said, ignoring the interruptions.

"Same," Logan said.

Winter pulled her knees under her and got comfortable. "I need a fresh start."

The questions stayed rapid-fire. The dragons didn't ask them to elaborate, only watched them carefully as they answered. What was their last job? Where would they be interested in working here? Where did they see themselves in ten years? Why hadn't they settled down with a mate yet? That was a hard one. They were supposed to keep answers simple, but Winter's murmured, "I had a mate, but he chose another," got a slew of questions from Dustin, then Emma, and even one from Beast.

The dragons never brought it back around either, just watched her uncomfortably expose her secrets until Winter wanted to crawl under a rock and hide for the rest of her life. Logan sat silently against the wall, pricking the edge of his thumbnail with a giant Bowie knife he'd pulled from somewhere.

"What's Brody's last name?" Logan asked carefully.

"No," Kane said sternly, power crackling across the single word.

Dustin relaxed on the couch beside Winter and looked into his pants. "I think Emma bruised my balls." He opened the front of his jeans wider and angled his hips toward Emma. "Do they look purple to you?"

Emma looked at a snickering Rowan with a dead-eyed expression as she shook her head. Dustin was exhausting.

"Winter?" Dustin asked. "Purple or no?"

"Show her your dick, and I'll kill you," Logan said on a sigh as he leaned his head back against the wall.

"What is with you, man?" Dustin asked. "You're all death threats and emo. Sex is supposed to put you in a good mood. Unless Winter's crotch is broken. It's not broken, is it? Asking for a friend."

Winter wanted to give him a second kick to the jewels but settled for shoving him in the head.

"Ow. Besides," Dustin continued, "if we become the new Blackwing Crew, we'll all see each other naked when we shift. I'm gonna put all your tiny wieners to shame."

Emma leaned over Winter's lap and looked down Dustin's pants with an impressed quirk to her lips. "Vienna sausage. Nice."

Winter burst out in a laugh, and even Logan, Rowan, and Kane chuckled. Beast stood against his wall with his arms crossed like he hated the world, and Dustin snapped his underwear back in place and argued that his dick was, "at least a bratwurst."

Winter was rolling now. God, today had been exhausting and partly terrible, funny, and overwhelming. Her arm hurt, she was hungry, and she should be mad as a hornet at Logan for what he'd done, but mostly she was relieved. Tonight she was listening to werewolf dick-jokes instead of drowning out Lynn and Brody's loud honeymoon fucking with music and the sound of her own crying.

Her giggles tapered off slowly. Maybe she was hysterical or emotionally exhausted, and this was the result. Whatever it was, the others were smiling, too, and she imagined it had been a long, hard day for all of them.

"This interview is done," Kane muttered, his smile lingering. "Same thing I told the others—if Rowan and I are still interested, we'll call you by ten in the morning. There's a motel ten miles down the road you can stay in, or you can go all the way to Bryson City for rooms if you want." The dragon jerked his chin toward the door and muttered, "Get out of my territory."

And as they filtered out of the cabin, something settled inside of Winter. Maybe it was the sunset that cast the sky in such pretty colors, or the lush greenery around Kane's land. Or maybe it was the chill she got when she brushed her knuckle over the lopsided house number, 1010. Or the sound of the others saying their farewells, or Logan's lingering glance over his shoulder at her as he made his way to his battered truck.

She couldn't put a finger on just one thing that made her feel so deeply comfortable in this moment, but down to her marrow, she knew this place was part of it.

And these people were important.

TEN

Winter felt better this morning than she had in a long time, which made no sense because she bore a new claw mark that still looked seven shades of awful. But whatever. The D-Team had already talked about it, along with Kane and Rowan, so what was the point of hiding it?

She'd actually brushed her hair today and piled it up on top of her head in a messy bun that, if she said so herself, looked cute with the actual make-up she'd applied and her aviator sunglasses.

The nerves were there, though, fluttering in her stomach like dry leaves in a stiff wind. As she laced up her boots over her skinny jeans, she checked the clock on the nightstand for the hundredth time this morning. It was 9:50, and still no call from the dragons.

What if she was out on the first round? Even with Ben vouching for her, what if she didn't make the cut? Then she would have to go back to Red Havoc with her tail tucked between her legs and settle into a life she couldn't imagine anymore. That, or she would have to search for another crew. But that put her hackles up because the dragons now knew the grit she'd gone through, and she really didn't want to explain that to another alpha again. Plus...Logan.

With a sigh, she stood and made her way out of her small motel room.

Logan was sitting outside of his room a couple doors down, his knees drawn up, arms resting over them and his phone dangling from one hand. He slid her a glance and, to her shock, a little smile that disappeared almost immediately. But it had been there. It counted.

"You get a call yet?" she asked.

"No, you?"

Winter shook her head.

Dustin appeared between two cars with a

massive sack in his hand. Grease stains at the bottom said whatever he'd brought was probably delicious. When the scent of Chinese food hit her nose, her stomach growled.

Without an invite, Dustin sat down next to Logan and started unloading little cartons of food from the bag. Beast was now making his way toward them from the other side of the motel parking lot, and Emma came out of a room about ten doors down.

Winter reached for a carton of noodles, but Dustin slapped her hand and said, "No," sternly like she was a dog taking from the dinner table. "You still owe me money from yesterday's failed food run."

Winter pulled out a wadded twenty from her pocket and threw it at him. It bounced off his forehead, but he caught it neatly and said, "You can have one bite. Don't give me mouth herpes."

Winter rolled her eyes and grabbed a pair of chopsticks from the pile of condiments he'd upended onto the sidewalk. Emma didn't even ask, just sat down and grabbed some fried rice. Beast sat on the curb a few doors down, glaring across the parking lot at another group of shifters from yesterday—the competition.

"Hey deaf girl," one of them yelled. "You get a call yet?"

"She can't hear you, dude," one of his friends said. The A-Team cracked up. High fives were exchanged, but Emma ignored them and kept her eyes on her food.

"What if I yell louder?" the idiot called. The others snickered again. "No? No call then?"

Winter wanted to claw their smirking faces off.

"Keep talking," Logan dared them. He smelled like fur.

"Okay. All six of us got calls an hour ago." The boastful B-hole gave one of his friends a high five and then cupped his mouth. "Looks like the handicap squad didn't make the cut."

"False," Dustin said nonchalantly. "I haven't got my call yet, so they aren't done with them. Kane's just trying to scare me. I know I'm in so not all the calls have been made."

Logan turned on his phone and glanced at the time that flashed on the screen. "You sure seem confident that Kane will call you back."

"Oh, I know he will."

"How?" Beast asked in a gravelly voice. Why

were his eyes glowing gold like his animal was riled up? No one was even threatening him.

Around a bite of eggroll, Dustin said, "Because I have something he wants."

"Blackmail?" Emma said. "Good luck with that angle. Kane'll burn you for trying."

Dustin snatched the carton of fried rice from her hands and glared at her, but Emma didn't even miss a beat, just grabbed another container of food and started eating that.

Winter liked her. Human she might be, and a little differently abled with her hearing, but Emma didn't take shit from anyone. Winter wanted to be more like her.

Beast's phone dinged and, a moment later, the other four phones chirped with text message alerts.

Looking borderline terrifying, Beast glared back at them. "Rejection?" he asked in a gravelly voice.

"Should we all check at once?" Logan asked quietly.

Winter sighed, so disproportionately nervous to what she should've been. It was just a crew rejection, not the end of the world. A few days ago, she hadn't even wanted to try for this crew. Why did everything feel so different now?

"One," Dustin drawled out. Then he opened his text and pumped his fist. "I'm in, suckers."

"I thought you were counting to three, asshole," Winter muttered as she navigated to the right screen.

A group text came up titled *D-Team*.

This is your call-back. We're doing more group interviews with the others over the next couple of days, but want to do something different with the D-Team. Horseback riding on Saturday. Smokemont Riding Stable at six and then dinner after. You guys were a hard no from Kane, but I'm pushing for you. Don't make me regret this.

Rowan.

"Horseback riding?" Logan asked. "No horse is gonna sit under me."

"Me, either," Dustin said, eyes narrowed at the screen of his phone.

Beast grunted. If Winter spoke caveman, she would guess he agreed with the other guys.

"That's the test, right?" Winter said. "To see if we can control our animals enough to ride a horse?" She was trying to stay positive, but the hard, cold fact was this was going to weed them out real quick.

Gesturing to the A-Team, Emma asked, "Why don't they have to do this? I'm human, and I can feel the bad vibes when I'm around them. They're all psychopaths like you guys."

"Thanks for the judgment," Dustin muttered as he shoveled another bite of noodles into his maw. "And what are you bitching about? You're human. You'll be fine on a horse."

Emma shrugged. "Maybe I don't want to be in a crew with the A-Team. A stands for asshole."

Dustin froze, noodles hanging from his mouth to his chopsticks. "I knew it. I didn't want this to happen, but you're falling for me. Should we bang now? I like doggy style."

"Screw you," Emma said, swatting his chopsticks.

When a noodle snapped and smacked Dustin in the face, Winter laughed. "Okay, so the horseback thing will be hard, but it's not a definite 'no' yet. At least we got a call-back."

"You're so positive," Dustin said. "And you washed your hair today. Is that actual lip gloss you're wearing? Winter, you don't look like a hobo. Sex with our resident lunatic did you good."

"Enough," Logan growled.

"You don't think she looks extra pretty today?" Dustin pushed. "She probably dressed up for you. Look, she even has your marks on display."

Winter sat frozen and mortified as Logan looked over at her arm. He winced and refused to agree with Dustin. The flush in her cheeks reached the tips of her ears.

"Fail," Dustin muttered. "I set you up nicely, man. All you had to do was call her pretty, and she would've let you put your worm in her slimy hole again. See if I help you get laid again."

Emma scrunched her face up in disgust. "God, do you know anything about women?"

"Uh, I know everything about women," Dustin said as a blob of fried rice fell out of his mouth.

Logan stood and made his way to his bashed-up truck.

"Where are you going?" Beast ground out as he passed.

Logan yanked the driver's side door open and muttered, "To the stables. I have to figure out how to ride a horse."

They all sat there frozen as Logan backed out of the parking spot. And just as he was about to pull away, he slammed on the brakes and rolled down his window. Leveling Winter with a bright-eyed look, he said, "Do you guys want to come?" in a snarly voice.

"I know Winter wants to *come*. Heyoooo," Dustin said, raising his hand for a high five that Emma did not return.

Winter was trapped in Logan's questioning gaze. He was so handsome in the morning light, so earnest in his invite, and even though he'd offered for everyone to come, it felt as if he was speaking directly to her.

Winter set her carton of food in the bag, stood, dusted off the seat of her pants, and then made her way to the truck.

"Shotgun!" Dustin called, scrambling to close lids and load up the food bag with the leftovers.

Fine with her. Winter got in the back seat with Emma, and to her shock, Beast opened the opposite door and climbed in the back with them. He took up damn near half the seat and barely got his seatbelt buckled.

So none of them were friends, and really, they

were each other's competition in a way. But this was a good idea. They knew the challenge coming, and if they could get a leg up and practice beforehand, maybe some of them would have a shot at staying.

Logan's gaze drifted to her in the rearview, and she smiled. She couldn't help herself. He made her feel all fluttery and happy, despite the chasm that yawned between them. He was a perfect distraction from her old life and intrigued her more than she was comfortable admitting. As they hit the main road, Emma rolled down the window and Beast cracked his knuckles like a barbarian. Dustin passed Winter's half-eaten carton of food back to her as he chattered on about how much better he would be at riding horses than the rest of them.

Winter propped her feet up on the console and bobbed her head to the rock song Logan had turned on.

If she really thought about it, this was terrifying, being shoved in a small space with these people. The marks on her arm still throbbed, and the memory of Logan's bear was still fresh. Beast felt like a maniac beside her, and Dustin's wolf would no doubt be just as broken as the rest of their animals. But Winter's alarm bells stayed silent, and her panther stayed calm inside of her—waiting and observing.

So they were the D-Team and a hard no from Kane, according to Rowan's message. They had an icicle's chance in hell at registering to the Blackwing Crew without the alpha backing them. At least they were still in the game, and at least they weren't just sitting around the motel hoping to squeak by the next round. This was a proactive bunch of monsters.

And suddenly something struck her. Before Brody, Winter had kept her eyes on tiny bright sides. That's how she'd survived, but somewhere along the way, she'd slipped into shadows and had lost sight of the positives. And now here she was, looking at the bright side again.

Winter gave a private smile. A few days out of Brody's shadow, and she was beginning to feel like her old self again.

Logan met her eyes in the rearview again, then shocked her silly when he reached back, gripped her ankle in his giant hand, squeezed gently, and said, "You look real pretty today."

Dustin went off on a pervy tirade, and Emma bumped her shoulder, but Winter couldn't take her eyes from the slight flush of red that crept up Logan's neck and landed in his cheek. He was embarrassed, but he'd said it anyway. He'd given her a compliment in front of everyone, and now her cheeks were heating, too, but not with embarrassment.

With pleasure.

ELEVEN

"This is a disaster," Logan muttered from where he lay on his back in a pile of warm horse shit.

His mighty steed was running full-speed away from Logan like he was in a race for the back gate of the massive corral. Beast was trying to approach a horse that had pinned itself into a corner out of fear and was kicking its back legs. Dustin was hunched over, clutching his arm, which looked to be pulled from the socket while his paint horse was charging after Logan's, and Winter was up on a bucking bronco, holding onto the saddle-horn for dear life while the handlers at Smokemont Riding Stables were trying to settle the beast.

Logan narrowed his eyes at Emma, who was

prancing around the arena like a goddamned professional barrel racer.

They were all screwed but the human.

A pretty blond in sparkly-pocketed jeans and a plaid button-up shirt offered her hand. "Let me help you up."

One, Logan didn't want to take his eyes off Winter right now, and two, he didn't much like touch. The mouse wouldn't have been able to lift him up anyway, so he stood on his own and dusted dirt off his jeans. The back of his T-shirt was rank, so he peeled it off carefully, but then realized his mistake when Blondie looked at him as though she wanted to shove one-dollar bills down his underwear. Fuck, he forgot how horny humans got over nudity, and now he was feeling vulnerable. Not enough to put the crap-stained shirt back on, though.

Winter's eyes flashed his way, and with a little scream, she dismounted. And by dismounted he meant she flung herself off the bucking horse and landed with cat-like grace on both feet. And now she was stomping his way like a sexy little hellion. Logan bit his lip against the accidental smile promising to wreck his face. If Winter's smoky-eyed glare was anything to go by, Blondie better run.

"I don't understand why the horses are actin' like this," she said to Winter as she approached. "We'll get y'all a refund, and maybe you can try to come back another day when the horses are settled. Maybe there's a snake slitherin' around their stalls, rilin' 'em up or somethin'."

Winter's smile didn't reach her eyes but she was polite as hell. She parted her lips as if she would say something cordial, but a harsh hiss sounded from her. Eyes wide, Winter clapped her hand over her mouth as Logan belted out a surprised laugh.

"This isn't funny!" Dustin called from where he leaned against the fence, all red-faced and sweaty. His arm was flopping around, obviously out of its socket, and now Beast was stalking him like a lion on an injured wildebeest. Shit.

Big old dominant shifters got some unfortunate instincts when they were around other injured predator shifters. Their animals wanted to attack. Hell, Logan was having trouble keeping his bear from ripping out of him and putting Dustin out of his misery right here in front of everyone. Too many human eyes on them, though, and he definitely didn't want to die of old age in some shifter prison.

"'Scuse us," he muttered, pulling Winter behind him. Hell, she seemed to be able to tame over-muscled, under-sexed dominants. She'd been working wonders on his bear all day and had kept him and Beast from murdering each other yesterday. She was basically a monster-whisperer.

Beast was getting closer to Dustin, walking faster, hands clawed up and eyes bright gold.

"Beast, stop!" Emma yelled from atop her bay horse.

Beast did not stop. In fact, he sped up as if he needed to attack before someone stopped him.

"No, no, no!" Dustin yelled, good arm out as he sidled down the fence.

Logan muttered a curse and sprinted to cut him off, was able to push him back and off-course but Beast was determined. For the effort, Logan got a fist to the freaking eye. Pain blasted through his skull, and he scrambled to hold onto Beast's waist. Squinting out of his good eye, he could see Winter struggling to pop Dustin's arm back into place. She was yelling at him to, "Stay still!" but Dustin was howling at the pain because Winter apparently didn't have a gentle touch when she was panicked.

"Hurry," Logan grunted, tackling Beast to the ground.

As he hit Beast across the jaw to try and rattle him out of his hunt, Emma sprinted by. Dustin was snarling too damn loud, and Winter was going to get bit. If Emma did, she'd be turned into a psychopath werewolf, so Logan barked out, "Emma, get back!"

She ignored him like a champ and held Dustin's good shoulder. She gestured to Winter, walking her through some professional-sounding steps to get the arm back in the socket as if she'd done it a hundred times.

Almost done.

Beast slammed him into the dirt and whaled on him, but okay. This was better than him murdering Dustin in front of these humans.

But his bear was enjoying this too damn much.

Kill him.

Logan shook his head hard to punish the animal, to dislodge the visions flashing across his mind of another battle—one where he'd challenged a head-sick tiger shifter and put him down. Troy. Troy's name was a black mark on his soul.

Beast's face morphed into the dark-haired tiger shifter's face that haunted his dreams, then back to Beast's face. To Troy's features, and then back.

Kill him.

Logan rolled them over again and pounded Beast's jaw, caught the titan's fist in his own and crushed his hand.

"Logan!" He could barely hear a woman's voice through the red fog that was seeping through his mind.

Someone touched him now, pulled at him. He didn't like touch. Logan yanked away so he could bash Troy's face in. He wasn't called in unless they'd taken innocent human life. He was justice. This asshole had killed. Troy wasn't able to control his animal, so Logan would control it for him, six feet under.

"Logan, stop!"

This was a good fight. Troy was an even match. Surprising. His alpha said he was middle of the crew dominant, but he'd been wrong. Troy was strong and dominant as hell, unbreakable...almost. Troy's face twisted up like the big cat that was inside of him, his teeth growing longer. White tiger or orange? One would show blood better. *Kill him.*

Troy was going to shift. Finally. Logan's bear knew the drill, no shifting until the target did. It had to be a fair fight so he could keep his sanity longer.

"Beast, don't Change!" someone screamed. Beautiful scream. She sounded scared as her claws scrabbled at his back.

Beast? No, this was Troy. Troy, Troy, Troy. Right? The man under him morphed. He changed to a scar-faced man with short blond hair and gold eyes. Lion eyes, not a tiger's. Not Troy's eyes.

"Logan, please." Winter. His Winter. Not cold like winter, but warm. Warm Winter. Winter of Nowhere.

The bear was right there, scratching at his skin, but Logan had to stop him. Logan took a hit to the stomach and doubled over, flung himself off Beast. Not a threat to humans, not a target. Just another broken shifter like himself.

When he coughed hard, blood sprinkled the arena dirt under him. Beast had gotten in some good lung shots. He wasn't in a jungle anymore, but the horse stables. Dustin was yelling at Beast, who was subdued now, looking as confused as Logan felt. Emma was heaving breath, pacing along the fence line. And Winter—beautiful Winter—was kneeling beside him, her hand gentle on his back as he coughed his lungs up.

He should be ashamed, but she didn't berate him. She was chanting, "It's okay. It's okay," offering him salvation with her words.

Her hand felt so good, petting him along his spine, with the grain of his fur if he was shifted right now. His head throbbed, stomach throbbed…dick throbbed. He wanted to bury himself in her again and feel better for a few minutes, but he remembered where he was and what he'd done. The marks from their first pairing were still deep and red on her arm.

Logan struggled up and away because the bear was too damn close to her. She wasn't safe enough.

She wasn't letting him away, though. She chased him all the way to the fence and cornered him, trapping him until he couldn't escape, and then she wrapped her arms around his back as if he wasn't a waste of space. As if he was worth something. Her lips brushed his skin over and over, right over his heart. What was she doing? It felt good, but she made no sense. She should be running. He could smell the fur of her animal, could smell her terror, yet here she was clinging to him.

"I want to be good enough," he muttered hoarsely, mindlessly. *Don't do that to her. Don't give her hope.*

"You are."

What she said made him angry. Logan struggled out of her grip and glared in shock at her. "You've lost your mind. Yell at me, Winter. Where is your anger?"

"Logan," Emma murmured.

She and Dustin were approaching now, herding him, but he wasn't some fucking sheep. "Stay back!"

Beast snarled from twenty yards away, but fuck it. Winter needed to hear this.

"I keep waiting for you to yell at me for what I did to you, Winter. You let me get away with something unforgiveable! I don't fucking get it! It's not okay. Nothing is okay, so stop telling me that. Don't be that girl who doesn't call people out on their shit. Don't be weak."

Winter looked so hurt. It was in the tears that rimmed her eyes. He hated himself.

"Maybe it takes a strong person to care about someone despite their monstrous faults," she gritted out as she strode past him, bumping his shoulder hard.

"I'm calling the police!" one of the handlers called from where he and the others were crowded in a loose group. He had a phone up to his ear. Shit.

The others drifted past him, making their way to the parking lot.

"Way to go, douchebag," Emma muttered.

Logan expected Dustin to make some smart remark as he meandered past rubbing his shoulder. He didn't, though. He kept his eyes averted, neck exposed, and murmured, "Thanks for that back there."

Logan huffed a breath and hooked his hands on his waist as he looked up at the blue sky above. He might have started off with good intentions on saving Dustin from Beast, but he'd ended it in psycho-land, flashing back to a kill. If they knew that, they would shun him from the D-Team, or whatever they were calling themselves. Something about that thought made his stomach hurt worse than the punches he'd taken to the gut.

He'd never cared about belonging before, so what was wrong with him now? Clearly, more desperation on his bear's part to save himself.

Beast glared at him from where he leaned on the fence, his face all bloody and bruised to hell. Logan spat red in the dirt and muttered, "Sorry, man." Then turned and made his way behind the others toward his busted-up truck.

This was why he didn't get close to people. No matter his intentions, he always hurt them. He made bad decisions. Winter had comforted him and hugged him when he felt like his insides were falling apart, and what had he done? Called her weak for it.

Another mistake to stomach on his way down. Winter wasn't weak at all. She'd fixed Dustin's injury and kept Beast from Changing and calling out Logan's inner bear. She'd approached him when he was midway to shifting, even though she'd been deeply and physically hurt by his bear before.

Dustin had thanked him for helping him, but the werewolf didn't understand.

Brave, beautiful, quiet, understanding Winter was the one who had saved them.

And something dark and selfish inside of Logan wished she could save him, too.

TWELVE

Winny, I'm worried. I miss you. Where are you? Ben won't tell me anything. I need you.

God, she'd always hated the nickname Brody had given her. Winter huffed a sigh and debated texting him back to leave her alone. But if she opened up a line of communication, he would dig in and get relentless, and what if she caved eventually? What if Logan had been right? What if she was weak?

Maybe she should change her number.

Her phone dinged again, and a flash of anger took her. He had a mate, a wife, a child on the way. He had the perfect life she'd always wanted, and he was throwing it away. She didn't want anything to do with his self-destruction.

She glared at the glowing screen, but bolted upright when she read the text from an unknown number.

I didn't mean what I said earlier.

Who is this, she messaged, just to make sure.

You know. You aren't weak, Winter. I am. Just wanted to say sorry.

She drew her knees up to her chest and relaxed against the headrest of the motel bed. The lights were off and the television was on but turned all the way down. She stared at the Old West shoot-out playing across the screen. Her heart rate was going a thousand miles a minute, and what did that say about her? Nothing good. Logan was bad news, but she'd still latched onto him deeply already.

How did you get my number?

Resources from the old job. That, or Emma gave it to me and told me to stop being a dick.

I like Emma, she typed with a smiley face.

If I had a heart, I would like her too. It was followed by a little grinning devil symbol.

Okay, so Logan knew how to tease. Good. Winter turned around on the bed and put her feet onto the wall facing his room, just to feel more connected to him. *Brody just texted me. I'm thinking about being super WEAK and messaging him to come cheat on his new pregnant wife with me. He might be my soulmate.* Devil symbol. Send.

A minute drifted by, and at last her phone dinged again. *Are you trying to get him killed?* Then the symbol of a harmless-looking teddy bear came through.

Winter giggled. *Are you in your room?*

Sitting outside in a bag chair that Dustin gave me. Drinking a six pack after the disaster that was today. Don't come out here. I'll fuck everything up in person. It's my way. This chair smells like wet dog.

Winter log-rolled off the bed and padded over to the window. With the barest brush of her fingertips, she moved the curtain just a crack. Logan was out there in a pair of dark gray sweatpants, no shirt, two beers into a six pack, staring at his phone like he was waiting for her to respond. His lips were curved up slightly. Then suddenly he looked over at her, right at her.

Winter squeaked and unhanded the curtain, bolted from the window, and laid on the bed again, feet up on the wall.

Her phone vibrated. *Curious kitty.*

She rested her hand on her stomach, right over the butterflies there, then typed her response. *So you know...I was really mad at you for the claw marks. Just because I don't react the way you think I should doesn't make me weak. I'm just tired of fighting with everyone, and I know you didn't mean to do it.*

A couple minutes passed. *I did mean to do it.*

Winter frowned. *Your bear did, but not you. You wouldn't hurt me. Right?*

Goodnight Winter.

And there it was. Logan cut people off who got too close to the real him, and this was his line. He'd drawn it in the sand, but it wasn't an invite to come over to his side and join him, no. His line was really a fence, and he was behind it like a rabid guard dog keeping everyone away from his junk yard. She could beg him to keep talking to her, but Logan didn't respond to pushing. He responded to patience. He *rewarded* her for patience with tiny peeks into his soul that he likely didn't share with anyone else.

Goodnight Logan.

She got up and looked out the window again, just to see him pack up, but he didn't. Instead, he buried his face in his hands and rubbed the heels of his palms against his eye sockets. The soft murmured, "Fuck," drifted through the window. Logan rested his elbows on his knees and shook his head for a long time as if he was at war with himself. He looked back at his phone, typed something in, then shook his head again and turned it off. He stood and started packing up, so she let the curtain fall again, her emotions completely mixed now.

Logan didn't feel so much like a distraction from Brody anymore. Logan was second to no one. She imagined him as a beautiful puzzle. She held two misshapen pieces in her hands, brightly colored, interesting, a fraction of the bigger picture that was Logan. She wanted more. She wanted to collect them all, one by one until she could really and truly see him.

He thought he was ruined, and maybe some of his pieces were.

Not all of him, though.

She could tell in the way he'd held her in the bathtub and how he'd stuck up for Emma today when the A-Team was popping off. She could tell because he'd invited the D-Team to ride horses just for a better shot at the crew. And in the way he hadn't hesitated to put himself between Beast and Dustin.

She could tell he wasn't ruined because of his apology.

Winter readied for bed in a daze of spinning thoughts. Logan was push and pull, and she didn't know how she felt about being constantly dragged up and down emotionally. But Brody had been solid from day one, and look what had happened. He'd been a secret monster all along. At least Logan owned his struggle.

It was cold in the motel, and the thermostat was one stubborn sonofabitch, so she pulled on an oversized, threadbare sweater and some knee-high socks and made down the sheets. But just as she moved to turn off the muted television, a knock sounded on the door.

Shifter she may be, but idiot she was not, so she peeked through the window before she opened the door. Logan stood there, looking at her, eyes glowing silver, arms locked against the doorframe. He looked terrifying. And delicious.

Slowly, she opened the door, then leaned her cheek on the edge of it. "More apologies?"

Logan shoved off the frame and retreated a couple steps, eyes never leaving hers. "Do you need more?"

"No."

He swallowed hard and ran his hand down his dark whiskers. "Can I come in?"

"Is this a booty call? Because last time we did the deed, I got some unfortunate body modifications."

His glance flitted to her arm covered with the sweater sleeve, then back to her eyes. "I won't push that, but..." He shrugged one shoulder up.

"I'm tired," she murmured.

He nodded. "Of course. Sorry."

He turned to leave, but she said softly, "You want to lay beside me?"

Logan halted, his back to her. His shoulders lifted in a painful looking inhale, as if he was having trouble breathing. "Yeah," he said low. "I want that."

"You ever done that before—just slept beside someone?"

He shook his head. He still wore his gray sweats and no shirt, so she could see how tense his back was. He looked like a stone, standing there in the halo of lamplight. Slowly, he turned, neck exposed as he passed her and stepped into her room.

"Smells good in here," he rumbled. "Smells like you."

She smiled and slipped her hand in his. He flinched but didn't pull away. After a split second of hesitation, he squeezed gently and looked down at her, the bright gray in his eyes cooling to a stormy color. He led her to the bed and waited for her to crawl in, then hit the power button on the television remote, casting them into complete darkness.

Winter held open the covers for him, grinning like a lunatic because Logan wanted touch. He wanted connection. With her. The butterflies turned to hummingbirds in her stomach as his warm leg rubbed hers.

"I like what you're wearing," he murmured. "Just the socks and shirt, no pants. You ever feel like sending a dirty pic, you take a selfie in that get-up for me, will ya?"

She giggled and snuggled closer, slid her hand over the flexed abs on his stomach. He stayed stiff under her, as if he didn't know what to do, but that was okay. Affection wasn't natural for a man like Logan. At least he was trying.

After a few minutes of his heartbeat pounding under her palm, Logan rolled toward her and slipped his arms around her, cradled her against his chest. He was shaking. "Am I doing this right?"

When a deep, rumbling purr vibrated her throat, Logan chuckled at her answer. "Winter?"

"Yeah," she whispered in an effort not to break the magic of this moment.

"What happened to you? I mean before Red Havoc. Why did your alpha have to save you?"

Now it was Winter who flinched. Logan plucked her clawed fingers from his ribcage and kissed the tripping pulse in her wrist gently.

She didn't want to talk about it, or revisit memories. She'd told Brody part of it, but he hadn't wanted to hear more. He'd told her he just wanted to look forward to the future, not get stuck in the past, so she'd pushed it all to the back of her head, locked it up tight so she wouldn't be a disappointment to Brody, who was normal and good and wouldn't understand baggage.

She'd been so desperate to be normal, too, it had seemed like a fair trade-off to pretend her life had begun the day she'd stumbled into Red Havoc.

But here was Logan, asking her to allow him into the shadows and let him have time to adjust his eyes to her darkness, and there was something so terrifying about that, but so liberating at the same time.

"My parent was human."

"Both of them?"

"No, just the one that counted. My mom was a panther, a drug addict, and she couldn't keep up with raising a kid, so she gave me to my dad. Signed away her rights, left him, left me. I only saw her a few times after that. She was…disappointing. My dad wasn't super well-off or anything, and we lived in New York, right in the middle of the city in this tiny one-bedroom apartment."

"You lived in the city?"

She huffed a breath. "Yeah. City shifter here, so you already know I'm fucked up. My animal was hard to control, and when I was a kid, I shifted as little as possible because I didn't trust my animal. My dad didn't like when I had to shift. He would drive me hours outside of the city and sleep in the car while I went on a little rampage through the woods once a month. He thought it was full-moon stuff, so that's when we went."

"Jesus," Logan murmured. "I can't even imagine keeping my animal inside a whole month."

Winter snuggled closer and shrugged her shoulders up to her ears. "It wasn't so bad when I got older because my dad found this underground job. A real hush-hush way for us to make money."

"How?" Logan asked in a dead voice.

"It was like a freak show." Her voice cracked on the last word, so she cleared her throat. She made her voice stronger as she continued. "I got to shift more in a controlled environment, and we made money."

"What kind of controlled environment?"

Shame heated her cheeks. "A cage. I was part of the show. People could watch me shift. I would slow it down so they could get more for their money. It hurt, but we got to move to a better apartment after a couple of years."

Logan was shaking again, but not from nerves this time. She could tell by the slow scent of rage that tainted the air.

She laid a gentle kiss on his chest. "It wasn't so bad. I went to school, and my dad was protective. I remember some pervert pulled down his pants and started jacking off during one of my shows, and my dad shut the entire thing down for a week, made new rules, beefed up security."

"He shouldn't have made you do that in the first place."

"Yeah well, it was his choice. And when I got older, it was mine, too. It was a steady income. It kept me in school and off the streets. The hard part was the way people looked at me though—like I really was a freak. It was hard to love myself during those years. Hard to accept the animal."

"So you spiraled?"

"No. That felt like nothing compared to the day my dad told me he was sick. He'd put off going to the doctor, I don't know why. I was mad at him, but we didn't have health insurance, and he just coughed more and more until I made him go. I guilted him into making the appointment because somewhere along the way, I think he forgot he was all I had. It was me and him against the world, you know? His lungs were sick, and it was bad. It was incurable."

"He died?"

Winter swallowed hard and shook her head against his shoulder. "I killed him. I read all the rules, and legally I could Turn one person. I picked my dad, but I didn't grow up with shifters. I didn't know how it worked. I just thought if I bit him, he would get better and be a panther shifter, like me. I thought I could save him." Winter's face crumpled, and she buried herself against Logan's chest at the memories of that awful day. "I waited until he was asleep one night. He'd had really bad coughing fits, couldn't breathe, was on an oxygen tank, and I thought if I bit him when he was on his pain killers, he wouldn't even feel my fangs. But apparently, you can't Change a sick person. You can Change an injured person, but they have to be healthy for shifter healing to work. You can't put an animal in a weakened host. And so he passed on his bed, and it was really bad." A sob wrenched up her throat. "It was an awful way to go. He loved me the best way he knew how, and I killed him."

"Shhhh." Logan rubbed her back in gentle circles.

Sobs wracked her body, and tears made damp spots on the pillow under her cheek. And when she could speak again, she whispered, "At least when you killed, it was people who deserved it. I killed the person I loved the most."

Logan hugged her tighter—so tight she could barely breathe, but she didn't care. It felt nice to be swaddled in his strength right now.

"I got to drinking, taking drugs, anything I could do to forget that night. I lost our apartment, started living on the street, begging for change so I could get the next fix of something just to go numb, you know?"

"What made you go find Red Havoc."

She laughed thickly. "Fate, I guess. My mom showed up at the subway where I was begging for money, and she was all strung out, mascara smeared all over her face, looking a hundred years older than she really was. My eyes are the same color, and I could see my future so clearly. I was going to end up just like her. She didn't say much. Just that she was sorry I lost my dad, and then she gave me this old, folded-up piece of paper. It was the location of a panther crew. She said she'd known about it for a while and was trying to get clean enough to join. She just..." Winter shook her head. "She just couldn't get her life together for long enough. She gave me fifty bucks and begged me to go see a man named Benson Saber. I had this moment when she was walking away. She'd never done anything for me in her entire life, but she'd just given me a second chance if I was willing to go after it. So I did. I hitchhiked out to Ben's crew three years ago and met Brody right away, detoxed, and went to work. I became a professional at pretending I was normal so I could fit in and be a good mate to Brody."

"And then he chose another."

Winter dipped her chin once. "Everyone leaves."

"If you truly believe that, then why are you here, trying for a spot in a crew?" he whispered.

"Because I guess I like the idea that maybe someday I can find my place, you know? My niche. Somewhere people will keep me. I didn't grow up in a crew, but I used to fantasize about the idea of one. I used to imagine I grew up with other kids like me, especially nights after a show when I felt so infinitely different than everyone around me. When I could hear the echoes of laughter and the sounds of disgust from the people who had watched my shift. I had this cork board in my closet with newspaper clippings from shifter articles. Pictures of the Ashe Crew, the Gray Backs, the Boarlanders, the Breck Crew. I liked the paparazzi pictures of the kids best, and I know it sounds so stupid, but I would pretend they were my friends, and I wasn't a freak, and I wasn't alone. I guess a part of me still wants that feeling of acceptance. I thought I found it with Red Havoc, but I didn't get the urge to register with Ben. I don't know why. My panther felt fine waiting. Maybe she saw Brody for what he was. Maybe she was just waiting for him to screw up. He was too perfect. Too clean. Perfect smile, perfect answer for everything, perfect hair, perfect place in the crew, and I was trailing behind trying to be good enough. I guess I'm trying for this crew because I still want to prove I'm good enough."

"If Kane doesn't choose you for the Blackwings, that's his loss."

"You think so?"

"I know so."

"How?"

"Because from where I'm sitting, you're the most incredible person. You've gone through so much, and you cleaned yourself up, picked yourself up, carved out a life."

"For Brody."

"Bullshit. You looked up to him as a guideline for normal because you didn't have that growing up.

You're here now, clean, happy, healthy, a secret strong-as-hell badass because of your own grit. Brody doesn't get credit for that. You do. You're enough, Winter."

She let off a long, shuddering breath at how good that felt to hear. It was a first. "Can you say that again?"

Slowly, Logan lowered his lips to her ear and whispered, "You're enough."

With a helpless sound, she eased her lips onto his as a thank you because he'd just given her something so important. Something she'd wanted for so long. She'd yearned for one person to feel like that, and it was him.

Logan froze under her lips, but she didn't care. She laid gentle pecs on him until his mouth softened against hers, and he kissed her back. This wasn't the match meets gasoline that had happened before. This was gentle sips and soft sucks and shallow nips. It was moving against each other and enjoying each other's taste, scent, feel.

He cupped her face and wiped her tears away with his thumbs, then slid his tongue past her lips. She loved the scratch of his beard against her soft skin and the way his hand went to her hip and squeezed as though he didn't want to ever let her go. She loved how he wrapped his strong arm around her head to keep her close. She loved how she couldn't feel his bear at all and Logan was giving her this beautiful moment without the risk of pain. She wanted it to last forever.

"Stay with me," she whispered against his lips.

"Winter," he murmured, easing away as if he would deny her.

She rushed onward. "Stay with me tonight. And tomorrow, stay with me then, too."

"I can't give you what you want. I can't be that for you. I'm not permanent."

Winter cupped his cheeks and kissed his denial away. "Give me one day at a time. I know you can do it. I was messed up, and I did it one day at a time, held onto the bright sides, clocked my progress, kept track of my little victories until I could get off my knees and stand on my own. And I'll be here cheering you on, Logan. Please. Just…don't quit."

"No more talking," he said low, and then his lips were on hers, more urgent this time. She could practically taste his desperation to escape her pleading. He slid his hand down her stomach and cupped his hand between her thighs.

Winter gasped and rolled her hips against his touch. She shouldn't encourage him. Sex with Logan got her hurt last time, but maybe if they just fooled around a little. The purr in her throat rattled louder, as if her panther had no survival instincts at all, and the human side of her was left all alone to make decisions about when to stop Logan.

When he slid his hand down the front of her panties, Winter gasped at how good his fingers felt sliding through her wetness. He circled her clit. Now her claws were out, digging into the back of his neck, keeping him close as he kissed her lips swollen.

"I won't hurt you," he whispered against her mouth, but she didn't miss the hint of a false note in his voice. He was trying to convince himself as much as her. "I *won't*," he said firmer, and there it was. He believed that one.

And as stupid as it was, so did she. Winter rested her leg over his hip. He inhaled sharply, dragged her hips toward him, and rocked his erection against her. He was so big, so hard, and his sweatpants so thin, she could feel the perfect outline of his shaft. She wanted that. Now.

She rolled her body gracefully against his, tempting him to touch her deeper, to touch her more, to ask for everything. His bear was here. He was in his mercury-colored eyes. He was in the scent of predator fur and the soft snarl in Logan's throat. His bear was here making the air feel heavy, but still, she didn't experience fear.

Her panther clearly had a death wish, and now Winter was at the mercy of her pheromones. Maybe Logan had been right. Maybe she was going into heat. She hadn't ever wanted anything or anyone more than Logan right now, and it made no damn sense because her arm was still sore.

Logan rocked them up until she was sitting on the edge of the bed with her back to him. She was confused for a moment before his hand slid her sweater slowly up her back. His fingers brushed her spine the entire way, and when her covering hit the floor, he didn't pounce, no. Logan pressed the flat of his palm on her shoulder blade and slowly dragged his hand down, raising gooseflesh where he touched her. He settled onto his knees behind her, easing her between his powerful thighs as he pulled her hair gently. When her head was angled to the side, his lips brushed her neck softly, like the stroke of a paintbrush. Behind her, his stomach and chest were rock-hard against her back, but his lips were pliable and easy on her skin.

A large mirror hung on the wall in front of her. Now that her eyes were adjusted to the dark, she could see him perfectly. He lifted those blazing silver eyes to their reflection and locked gazes with her. He looked wild and sexy, his shoulders flexing as he ran his hands down her arms. He opened his jaw wider, as if he would bite her, but he didn't. His nip stayed gentle and pleasurable on the side of her neck, right under her ear. Oh, he knew her buttons. It was male panther instinct to bite the back of the neck during sex, and it was just as erotic to the females. He was working her neck until she hadn't the strength to deny either of them.

Her chest heaved as he dragged his hand up her ribs and cupped her breast. Already, her nipples were drawn up in tight, wanting buds. Winter moved to take off her gray knee-high socks, but he pulled her hand away and shook his head. "Leave them," he murmured against her skin. He hooked a finger under the elastic of her panties. "These can go."

She couldn't help the smile on her face as she slid them down her thighs to her knees, ankles, then floor. Logan liked the socks. Noted.

He pulled her back on the bed and slid his hands between her closed knees, pushed them open slowly. His eyes blazed brighter when her sex was exposed to the mirror. Around her hips, his thighs clenched, and he rolled his erection against her back. Logan moved to kiss the other side of her neck. His hand slid down between her legs again. Without hesitation, he slid his middle finger inside of her. Shocked at how perfect it felt, Winter reached over her shoulders and gripped his neck as she writhed.

"God, you're so fucking sexy," he said on a breath as he watched himself finger her.

With a smile, she closed her eyes and rolled her hips against his touch again. He could watch all he wanted, but she just wanted to *feel* him right now. His lips on her neck, his finger buried inside of her, two now, his hard body against her back, his thighs encasing her… God, she loved this. Loved him. Loved him? Impossible. He was too new to her life, too dangerous.

Perfect.

No. Logan wasn't perfect, and it was dangerous for her panther to think that. He was flawed and broken just like her.

He matches us.

Desperate to push the panther from her mind, she turned in his arms and straddled his lap.

Logan didn't flinch or hesitate, but instead pulled her hips hard against him and trailed biting kisses down her arm over the claw marks. They tingled under his lips, under the scratch of his facial scruff. And then he was on her mouth again, kissing, biting, sucking, cupping the back of her head as their bodies moved together.

She couldn't think. Her body and mind belonged to Logan now, and with trembling fingers, she pushed the waist of his sweats down his hips. He lifted off the bed enough for her to maneuver them down to the middle of his thighs to unsheathe him completely. She rocked against his dick and groaned mindlessly as he reached between them and positioned himself at her entrance.

In a final, barely-there wisp of self-preservation, she pleaded, "Don't hurt me after."

"You don't understand," he gritted out, pushing deep into her. "I can't hurt you anymore. You're safe."

Safe. What a beautiful lie.

She eased off his cock and lowered herself onto him again until he was buried completely. A snarl rattled his chest, but she gripped the back of his hair and yanked his gaze to hers. The sound died in his throat when he looked at her, pupils blown out as though she'd short-circuited him. Good. At least this part of him wasn't broken either. Dominant or not, he could still be guided. As she rolled against him again, he leaned forward and kissed her, hand cupped on her cheek, fingers digging into her neck as they moved together.

God, he felt so good inside of her. The perfect fit. *Our match.*

Winter snarled, and against her lips, Logan smiled. She knew if she reared back and looked at him right now, it would be a wicked grin. He liked her animal. She could tell. He was so damn pleased with himself right now, she could practically feel the satisfaction wafting from his warm skin. So she let the cat have her fun, let her growl like she wanted while Winter kept him buried deep, only allowing him small thrusts.

"Fuck," he said in a feral voice, and she got it. She was close, too.

Logan buried his face against her neck and crushed her to his body, rolling his hips faster, crashing into her. His teeth grazed her neck over and over, but he never pushed to bite her. Never pushed to claim her. A terrifying part of her wanted him to. She wanted him to sink his teeth into her and anchor his bear to her animal. She wished he would bind them so he would have a harder time leaving this world. A harder time leaving her. But he didn't. His teeth scraped her skin, but never pierced it.

The pressure in her core was building with every stroke, and she was already toeing the edge of ecstasy. She was standing on the edge of a cliff about to lose herself completely in the free-fall and dive into the cool blue waters below.

She cried out with every stroke. Logan's fingers dug into her thighs as he rammed her hips with his.

The first pulse of orgasm shattered her body, and Logan yelled out her name and arched his neck back. Her quick pulses were met by the deep jerk of his dick, and then warmth, warmth, warmth each time their bodies met.

His release spurred hers on, encouraging more aftershocks than she thought possible. She and Logan slowed the pace, swayed together as the pleasurable throbbing sensation in her middle became softer. His lips were gentle again, and for some reason it made her want to cry. Logan wasn't on the attack tonight. He was massaging her thighs, brushing his fingertips up her back, gripping her neck gently, stroking her cheek, kissing her softer and softer, adoring her, all unrushed. Tonight, his monster slumbered and allowed her this breathtaking moment.

This was such a beautiful gift after yesterday's pain.

Logan huffed a soft sound, half-growl, half laugh. A smile curved his lips, and he shook his head as he stayed locked in her gaze. "I can't...I can't believe..." He eased back against the mattress, dragging her with him, and then curled around her body protectively. "He's fine."

As Logan smoothed her hair out of her face, she pecked his hand. "Your bear is okay?"

"Well, not okay, but quiet."

"Can I tell you something, and you not freak

out?"

"You can tell me anything."

"For a second there, I thought you were going to claim me."

The smile slipped from his face so fast his ears moved. He pulled the pillow under them better and rested his cheek just inches from hers. As quiet as a breath, he asked, "Would you hate that?"

Winter shook her head slowly, allowed him to see the steadiness in her eyes.

Logan swallowed hard in the quiet darkness and ran his fingertips along the sore claw marks on her arm. He followed his touch with his gaze, then blinked slowly and lifted those blazing silver eyes back to hers.

He didn't say anything, but that single look in his eyes said so much. She felt struck by lightning. Suddenly, everything made sense. His bear's attack, him promising he wouldn't have killed her, his protectiveness, his inability to leave her alone, his need to touch her tonight.

Her throat got so tight she couldn't speak right away, and her eyes misted with tears. "You didn't hurt me tonight," she croaked out emotionally.

"I told you I can't hurt you anymore."

Oh my gosh, oh my gosh, oh my gosh!

"Are these...?" Winter pressed her hand on top of Logan's, flattening his palm against the new scars on her arm. "Are these claiming marks?"

Logan looked sick and ripped his gaze away. "I'm sorry."

As he buried his face against her chest, she stared at the headboard above them. Claiming marks, the only way his monster knew how. It hadn't been sweet or in an intimate moment. It had been violent and forced and animalistic. It had been so...Logan.

"You didn't cover Brody's mark," she whispered, her head spinning.

"He's part of your history. Fuck his mark. I had to give you another one just from me. It wasn't a reaction to seeing Brody's mark. It was my bear choosing and me not working hard enough to stop him. And now I'm tied to you. I didn't ask you, though, and I know what this is. I can see it. It's okay."

"What do you think this is?" she whispered, stroking his hair. The tears streamed down her face, and her heart pounded like thunder.

"I take your mind off Brody."

Winter huffed an emotional laugh and inhaled raggedly. "You're no one's replacement, Logan."

"You forgive me?"

"On one condition."

"What?"

"You promise me day by day." Nope, she wasn't giving up on him like he had on himself. If he felt strong enough to claim her, he could get strong enough to stick around. She knew it. She believed in him, no matter what damage he or his bear had sustained. "Promise me."

He was quiet for so long she thought he would refuse to answer completely. But at last, with a huffed sigh, he cradled her closer and murmured, "Day by day."

THIRTEEN

Winter now knew what that song "Walking on Sunshine" was talking about.

For the second day in a row, she'd put on make-up, fussed over her hair, and turned into a grinning idiot every time she saw herself in the mirror. It wasn't vanity, but rather joy that she was finding her old self again. That and the giant hickey Logan had gifted her. And the marks. The *claiming* marks!

It was September, and chilly outside, but she was mighty tempted to wear a tank top again just so Logan would get that red flush to his cheeks and smile down at his feet like he'd done this morning before he left for his room.

These last five months she'd lived like a zombie,

meandering from one task to the next, numb and mindless. Not today. And if she was honest, she had been on an upswing from the moment she set foot on Kane's territory and met Logan and the D-Team. What a horridly dysfunctional batch of beasties they made, but Winter kind of liked it. None of them were angels, or even very safe to the human populace, and half the time they all drove each other bat-guano-crazy, but Winter was still protective over them in ways that surprised her.

She hoped they all made it into the crew.

But...what if they didn't? What if she didn't? What if Logan didn't? Or what if one of them made it, but not the other? Or what if she and Logan made it, but not Beast, Emma, and Dustin? Or what if Dustin and Beast made it, but not Emma and— *Stop it!* She would drive herself nuts with this train of thought. Whatever happened from here, she had to trust the process and the dragons to build the best crew for them and for the territory.

A knock sounded at the door. It was the polite sort, and since Winter had propped it open with the door latch, she called out, "Come in."

Emma pushed open the door and plopped onto

the unmade bed as Winter continued folding up the clothes she'd discarded in her insane search for the perfect outfit.

"Dustin's hungry for bacon." Emma frowned up at the ceiling and fiddled with her hearing aid. Maybe her voice sounded off or something, but to Winter, Emma sounded the same as always.

"Are we all going to breakfast?" Winter asked.

Emily rolled her head toward her, and her frown deepened, so Winter repeated, "Are we all going to breakfast?" careful to keep her face angled toward her so Emma could read her lips, too.

"Dustin said he's tired of hanging out with us."

Winter snorted. "Bullshit, why would he tell you he was hungry then?"

"Exactly. He got grumpy and yelled that he isn't waiting more than ten minutes for everyone, and then he slammed his room door like a spoiled princess. You ready?"

"Is Beast going?" Winter asked carefully. She was really working up to asking about Logan.

"He's already in the truck looking like he wants to kill everyone."

Winter giggled, then cleared her throat and tried

for aloof. "So Logan's going, too?"

Emma rolled her eyes and shook her head. "You two are ridiculous. You know he is a psychopath, right?"

"But he's *my* psychopath," Winter whispered through a grin as she folded the last shirt.

Emma pointed to her eyes and then to Winter's lips. "Nice try, I read that."

"I'm hungry for pancakes," Winter said, sidling Emma's gently kicking legs and grabbing her purse off the chair.

"Nice subject change," the honey-haired wood sprite said as she followed her out the door. "Are you looking for a job yet?" she asked.

"Not yet," Winter said, making sure Emma could see her lips. "I wanted to wait until I have a better instinct on how the dragons feel about me. I don't want to get my hopes up too high, you know? You?"

"Yeah, I put my application in at a coffee shop this morning. If this is going to take months, I can't afford the motel for that long. It adds up."

Logan and Dustin were arguing in the front seat of Logan's truck. Beast had evacuated it completely and was sitting in the bed, head leaned back on the side like he was sleeping.

Logan's angry voice drifted through the closed window. "I swear to God, Dustin, if you touch that radio dial again, I'm gonna gut you."

When Dustin leaned forward to poke the dial, Logan grabbed his finger. Dustin grinned and made a fart sound, and Logan roared in his face. This was how the day was going to go. Winter could just see it.

When Emma threw open the back door, Dustin yelled, "Bacon!" like it would make them hurry faster.

Winter put on her sunglasses so he wouldn't see her infinite number of eye-rolls today.

The reek of dominance made it crystal clear why Beast had evacuated, and immediately after buckling her seatbelt, Emma opened her window plus the back sliding window.

"Morning, Beast," Winter said cheerfully.

"No to all of your morning-person bullshit," he said blandly, not even bothering to open his eyes.

Winter shrugged her shoulders up to her ears and murmured, "He loves me."

"I love nothing," Beast said.

Dustin was fiddling around with the radio again, Logan was snarling like he was on the verge of a shift, and Emma was hanging her head out the window as though she—a dull-sensed little human—could feel all the monster-crap happening in the truck.

They would make the worst crew in the whole world. Winter's smile took over her whole face until her cheeks hurt.

"Stop smiling like that," Dustin said, looking eked out. "It's weird. And is that a hickey? Shit Logan, sex is supposed to put you in a good mood!"

Logan gritted out, "I'm not listening to techno all the way to the restaurant. It makes me feel crazy."

"Newsflash, asshole," Dustin said, slamming his back against the seat and crossing his arms. "You *are* crazy."

"I like your smile," Logan said, his eyes on Winter in the rearview mirror. He wasn't even close to grinning, his eyes were the color of a bug zapper, and his voice was terrifying, but she still got butterflies.

"I like your smile, too."

"Bacon!" Dustin yelled, way too loud. They all hunched their shoulders at the sound except Emma, who looked to be fighting back an amused grin.

Their phones all dinged with different tones, all seconds apart.

Dustin struggled his phone out of his pocket first. "Want me to read it?"

"Depends. *Can* you read?" Emma asked.

Winter pulled her phone out and read along as Dustin narrated. "D-Team, we got a visit from the police early this morning about a disturbance at the horse stables, complete with security footage of you idiots fighting."

"Oh, shit," Logan muttered.

"Because of this, all the shifters in the Smoky Mountains have been formally banned from the stables for a minimum of one year, and thus we cannot conduct your next interview as we'd planned. Please make your way to my mountains at your earliest convenience. That means now, D-Team. Kane."

"I like when Rowan texts us better," Winter murmured. "She's nicer."

"What is there to be nice about?" Beast growled from the back of the truck. "We left the arena splattered with blood."

"No, you and Logan did," Dustin pointed out. "I bled zero percent."

"Are we getting cut?" Emma asked, her green

eyes round as dinner plates.

"Probably," Beast said, louder than before. One look back at the bed, and he was red-faced, which made the gold in his eyes look even more terrifying. Fantastic.

"I seriously can't believe I threw in with you bunch of psychos," Dustin said. His eyes were glowing two different colors, and he smelled like fur. "I was in! I had all the cards, and now I'm going to get cut from the crew because of you guys!" He jammed a finger at Beast. "You suck." He jammed his finger at Emma. "And you suck, too." He pointed his middle finger at Winter. "And you suck the most—ack," he croaked as Logan tightened his fist around Dustin's throat.

"Don't fucking talk to her like that."

As Beast reached through the back window with a massive paw, apparently scrabbling for Dustin, Emma cursed them all out while beating on Beast's massive arm with both fists.

"Stop!" Winter yelled. Winter shoved Beast's arm as hard as she could. "Logan, unhand Dustin's throat, Dustin, stop being a chode, Emma, you're awesome, never change. We don't know what is happening yet or even if we are cut for sure, but I know one thing. We're all hungry and tired, and we shouldn't go up to Kane's Mountains on empty stomachs. Let's put in our to-go order and go find out what is really going on. Logan!"

With a growl, Logan released Dustin, who immediately jammed a middle finger in Logan's face and nearly got it bitten off. The wolf shifter removed the bird one millisecond before Logan snapped his teeth with a *clack*.

Emma was laughing again.

As Logan backed out of the parking spot, there was such a heavy, awkward silence it put Winter's hair on end. It was going to suck if it was like this all day.

As they passed the opposite side of the motel, the A-Team was gathered outside of one of the rooms talking low. When they caught sight of Logan's truck, they all stopped their conversation, and each of their lightened eyes drifted to them. They weren't joking this morning, and really, they looked suspicious as hell.

"Anyone find it odd that they've been doing that shit all morning?" Logan asked as they coasted by.

"I can find out their names if you want to murder them all," Dustin said. Apparently the wolf had caught wind of Logan's last profession, and there was this loaded moment that hung in the air, clogging up Winter's lungs as she waited for Logan's reaction.

"Careful dog," Logan said coolly. "I know your secrets, too."

"Okay, you caught me," Dustin said sarcastically. "I hold the world record for most masturbations in one day. Autographs later."

Beast snorted behind them, and Emma shook her head at Winter, eyes exhausted as if she needed a nap already.

But when Dustin turned up the techno music again, Logan didn't even yell at him, and that was some true and serious progress with this bunch. The awkward silence lifted, and Winter's smile was back to stretching her face.

Logan had claimed her, Kane hadn't come out and said they were eliminated, she was about to get pancakes, and she was in a truck full of her people.

Bright sides.

FOURTEEN

Kane was pissed. Logan could tell from the moment he drove across the territory line of the dark dragon. There was a vibration in the air that settled in his chest and made him sick to his stomach. He and everyone in this truck were insane for wanting to be a part of his crew.

He pushed the brake, unable to help himself. He couldn't make himself take Winter any closer to the angry Dark Kane.

"Go, man," Dustin said around a mouthful of French toast. "The later we are, the angrier he'll be."

"Do you feel it, too?" Logan asked.

"Of course I do, I'm not a pup. He's mad. He'll get over it and probably not burn us. He's got Rowan to steady him, or however bonds work. Find your balls and hurry the fuck up."

Logan growled, and a vision of him slitting Dustin from throat to belly button flashed across his mind. *Kill him.*

Feeling helpless for the first time in his life, he looked at Winter in the rearview.

"It's okay," she murmured, shoving the door open.

"What are you doing?" he asked as she got out.

The door shut hard, rocking the truck, and then Winter was in his window with the prettiest smile that existed on earth. Her smoky-gray eyes were all done up with dark eye-shit girls liked to slather on. Looked sexy on her. The lip sparkles on her smile did, too.

"You can't take me farther." She leaned her cheek against his elbow, which was resting on the open window frame. She nuzzled it like an affectionate cat and murmured, "I'll walk from here."

Well, that would solve the ache in his chest if she took herself to Kane, and it double-helped when Beast jumped out of the back of the truck and muttered, "I'll walk, too. Want to get there before my ninetieth birthday." Beast lurched at the window, but nothing scared Logan anymore, so he sat there watching him with dead eyes.

Beast lumbered away to leave Winter to trail after him, but she turned and bolted back to the truck, pecked Logan on the lips, grinned, stunned him completely, then strode off behind Beast, her sexy curves swinging like she knew he was watching.

Dustin licked his fingers loudly, dragging Logan from being damn-near hypnotized by her sexy ass. Winter waved as she walked away, and Beast flipped them all off. God, they really were the D-Team. All but Winter. She was the best person he'd ever met. He hoped her goodness rubbed off on his soul and smudged out some of the darkness. Selfish, but meh. He was a selfish monster and had accepted that long ago. The proof was in how little effort he'd made to stay away from her. There was a one-hundred-percent chance he was going to ruin her life, yet here he was, digging in deeper with his mate every chance he got.

His mate? Shit, that was an unexpected gem. He wasn't supposed to have one. Oh, he'd seen his destiny bright and clear from age seventeen. Winter wasn't supposed to be a part of it, but here she was, dragging him kicking and screaming into the light. *Day by day*. Logan shook his head and hit the gas on the bridge over the river.

That woman saw the good in everything, and everyone. Made no sense after all she'd been through, but thank God she was stronger than he was.

His stomach soured with every inch he drove toward Kane's cabin. This felt like more than just anger over a fight at the stables. It was too disproportionate. Shifters fought. So what?

He parked in the yard, and they piled out. Dustin dry-heaved in the side yard, which meant he was feeling the darkness as bad as Logan was. Emma even looked worried and was rubbing the gooseflesh on her arms.

Logan wanted to wait for Winter because he didn't like her out of his sight when the danger was level-red like this. But Kane yanked open the door and barked out, "Get in here."

Dustin muttered a curse and flashed Logan a worried look before the wolf led the way into the lair of the dark dragon.

Kane locked his arms on the kitchen table and

glared at the cell phone he had resting on the polished surface.

"Are you even listening to us?" a deep voice asked over the speaker phone.

A threatening rumble emanated from Kane and rattled the house. "Careful," he warned.

"You're too loud, too out there. You aren't the only shifters in the Smokies, dragon. And I'm not just talking about the Bloodrunners. There are families there who have kept their lives small and out of the limelight for years, and then you drag all the fucked-up monsters of our species to you? The media is making our home into a circus. Get rid of them."

The line went dead, and Kane chucked the phone at the wall in a blur. Emma winced as the phone exploded against the wall.

"Who was that?" Dustin asked, the humor drained from his voice for once.

"That would be Seth and Kyle of some Fuller Crew I didn't even know about, who apparently have family too damn close to my territory for comfort."

Winter and Beast walked in, stepping carefully and silently to stand beside Logan. Big cat shifters could do that, slink around without moving a single dust mote.

Kane rested his hands on his hips and glared at the floor, chest heaving. "Just so everyone knows, I didn't want this. I didn't want the attention. For fuck's sake, I was hidden for most of my life, and now I'm under a magnifying glass. Now I have to manage the media, other shifters in the territory, and pick the right damn crew. I can barely manage my dragon! And now I'm supposed to be a good alpha?"

Yep, Kane was freaking out.

Looking exhausted, Rowan stood in the kitchen, her back resting against the counter, arms crossed over her chest. "You will be a good alpha," she murmured low.

"I second that?" Logan said, lifting two fingers in the air. "You seem to care about being a good alpha a helluva lot more than my last alpha did. Victory."

Kane narrowed his eyes to furious little slits. "Winter Donovan, can I see you in my office?"

When Dustin dry-heaved again, Logan almost felt bad for him. He was the most submissive one here, and a pissed-off alpha did a number on low-ranked animals. Rowan brought him a small wastebasket and told him to, "Put your head between your legs. It'll get better when he settles down."

"You better not puke in here," Emma said. "Cowboy up, werewolf."

"Shut up," Dustin muttered, looking green around the edges.

Winter followed Kane down a hallway, but turned at the door to the office and cast Logan a worried look.

"You want me to go with you?" he asked immediately, his protective instincts blaring.

"I wouldn't," Rowan murmured softly.

She wasn't all smiley and supportive today. In fact, she looked about as green as Dustin right now.

"What's wrong?" Logan asked.

"I'm disappointed."

"About the fight at the corral?" Emma asked. "They didn't mean to. It's just their natures. The horses weren't cooperating, Dustin got hurt, and then Beast wanted to kill him, but it was like…soft murder, and we fixed it. I mean, Logan and Beast beat the everlovin' shit out of each other, but nobody died." Emma shrugged. "So that's good."

"I don't care about the fight," Rowan said. "I care about Kane." Her eyes had gone hard on Logan, as if he'd done something wrong. But when he opened his mouth to ask, Winter came back out of the office looking completely dazed.

"What's wrong?" he asked. And why did he feel like Changing? She didn't seem to be in danger, but his bear wanted to protect her from what? Dust bunnies and Dustin's dry-heave germs? *Get a grip.*

Winter lifted a small stack of papers and dragged those pretty gray eyes to his. They were full of some emotion he didn't understand. "I was invited to register with the Blackwing Crew."

"Great!" Dustin said, hugging his trashcan to his chest. "Blackwing invites. I'll go next."

"No, you won't," Kane ground out from where he leaned on the wall at the lip of the hallway. "No more invites are being offered."

Rowan wouldn't meet their eyes, and neither would Winter.

"I don't understand." Dustin stood. "Are you inviting the A-Team then?"

"No, I'm good with one crew member at this time," Kane said, as his eyes flashed with some deep anger at Dustin. "I know who you are." He arced his inhumanly bright gaze to Beast. "And you." He did the same to Emma and then to Logan. "And now I know who you are."

"From one grainy video of a fight?" Dustin asked.

Kane's eyes hadn't left Logan yet, and now he had the urge to back to the door or fight. His bear was having trouble settling on one.

"Kannon Dayton," Kane clipped out. The last name tapered into a snarl, but Logan had understood him well enough. The name felt like a fist to the stomach.

He shook his head, backed up a few steps. He didn't understand what was happening, but he sure as fuck understood Kane was angry. With him.

Kane stalked him slowly. "Kannon Dayton, Logan. Tell me how you knew him. *Fucking tell me!*" he roared.

Logan flashed a look at Winter who was moving to stand between Logan and Kane. He shook his head in warning. God, he didn't want to do this. Not in front of her. Not in front of anyone. Kannon Dayton was the reason he broke.

"My alpha gave me a job. A quiet one. There wasn't much money involved, but he told me it was important."

"Who hired you?" Kane gritted out.

Logan ignored the question because he hadn't said enough to make him understand yet. "When I got out there, to this rundown cabin in the middle of nowhere, I was confused. It wasn't how I usually did things. Kannon was alone, unregistered, and he felt like a wolf, but said he couldn't shift."

"Who hired you?"

"Kane, stop!" Logan held out his hand to keep the approaching dragon back. His bear was clawing at his insides now, chanting *kill him, kill him, kill him*.

"It's not the kind of job I did, but Kannon was bad off. Kept talking to himself, crying, smelled sick, told me he wanted to kill anyone in his territory and had almost taken a hiker's life. Told me he'd lost his animal, and he pleaded with me... Fuck... Kane, I don't want to do this."

"Who hired you?" he bellowed in Logan's face.

Kill him, kill him. Kill him for challenging you.

Logan closed his eyes against the pain of his bear trying to force a Change. "He did."

"What?" Kane shook his head, stumbled back a step.

"He hired me. Kannon did, but I didn't take the

money. I couldn't. He hired me to take his life because he'd tried twice and failed, and he wanted it over with. He couldn't Change, didn't have the wolf, so I couldn't kill him the way I wanted. I took his life because he fell to his knees in the dirt and clung to my jeans and begged me to." Logan slammed his head back against the door three times to rattle the bear out of control. He didn't even recognize his voice right now. *Kill him.* "And then I wasn't okay to keep going because I took a fucking human's life. He was basically a human, right? He smelled like a wolf, but his eyes were stuck glowing like a demon's, and he couldn't Change. He was empty. A shell without his animal, and I couldn't say no. I couldn't just leave him there like that, alone, dead inside but not on the outside." His eyes blurred and burned. Fuck! Everything hurt. His head, his heart, every muscle as he strained not to let the monster loose in a house full of people he actually gave a shit about.

"Was it Kannon's death that broke your bear?" Kane said, eyes narrowed with hatred.

"Yes," Logan gritted out, clenching his fists against the urge to Change and kill everyone.

"Good. He was my friend. He was in Apex. They

cut his wolf from his body like he was some fucking science experiment. He had a chance—"

"He didn't," Logan said. "You didn't see him, Kane. Didn't feel what he was like at the end. There was no recovery for him."

"You killed my friend!" Kane barked out. "And then you had the balls to come to my territory and ask the same goddamned favor he asked of you? You want to end it, Logan? You want that quick death? You want it over with? You've got it."

"No, no, no," Winter said, pulling at Kane's arm.

"Tomorrow night, six sharp, be here for your end, or I'll hunt you down like the animal you are. Everyone get out." Kane jerked out of Winter's grasp and strode for the back door.

It slammed so hard the house rattled.

Rowan murmured low, "He really loved the people he was in Apex with. Really loved them. They're experience bonded them in a way you or I or anyone can't understand." She dragged dragon-gold eyes to Logan and shook her head as twin tears spilled down her cheeks. "I don't want this, and I wish you hadn't asked for it. I wish you wouldn't have come to us. I wanted you in the crew, not to be a black mark on Kane's heart." She dashed her hand under her cheeks quickly and made her way into the hallway, shoulders shaking in silent sobs.

A prehistoric roar shook the house so hard a trio of decorative plates fell off their wall stands and shattered on the floor.

Feeling completely numb, Logan followed the others out of the house. Kane had said yes. He was going to give Logan his wish, but now something inside of Logan wanted to flee. A pathetic part of him clung to the idea that he could change eventually, improve, and be worthy of Winter.

Winter slid her arms around his waist and sobbed against his shirt. She was getting tears everywhere. The sun was too bright, too harsh. Logan's head was splitting in two. In the clearing beyond, Kane's dragon stood much taller than the cabin. He stretched his gargoyle wings and lifted off the ground with powerful strokes. The wind under his wings was like a tornado, and Logan struggled to keep Winter upright. Dark Kane was a true monster—hideous and terrifying. The spikes down his back shone like weapons, and his black scales were matted and scarred as if he'd battled for centuries to survive. Long, black horns arched out of his face, and his claws were monstrous.

Kane was true to his nickname—the End of Days.

At six o'clock tomorrow, Dark Kane was going to be the end of Logan's days.

Logan tightened his arms around Winter's shaking shoulders as he watched the massive dragon break through the cloud layer above and disappear from sight.

Now, after working toward the end for so long, Logan suddenly wasn't ready.

FIFTEEN

"There will be no pulling Kane off this, Winter," Ben said in a gruff voice. "Don't yank the tail of the dragon. Live."

Winter rested her cheek on the chain of the playground swing and swayed back and forth slowly. She'd thought Brody had broken her heart, but if Kane killed Logan, something inside of her said she would never be okay again.

"Ben, I care for him." Her voice came out tear-soaked and pathetic, but she was past caring right now.

"Winter, I know. I can tell, but you don't want a war with the End of Days. Trust me. I was in Apex for eight months with him. He was a friend, but one of the few people who ever really scared me. Not the human parts of him. The Blackwing Dragon parts. He's giving Logan what he asked for. He's giving him what he wants."

"But it's not what I want!"

"That's right, so I think we need to revisit that because I remember sitting down with you while we were drying you out, while you were detoxing and so sick and we didn't know if you were even going to make it. And I asked you what you wanted because I thought it would give you a reason to stay in this world, and do you remember what you said?"

Winter sniffed. "That I wanted a family who wanted me back. A family who stayed."

"Exactly. You pick the wrong people, Winter. You can see they're not right for you, deep down you can tell, but you cling to them anyway."

"You think Logan is a bad bet?"

"I think you've seen a different side of Logan than the rest of the world has seen. And I applaud you for trying to see the best in everyone. But I knew about Logan Furrow long before he went to Kane. I'd heard about him. An assassin for hire who had been trained to feel nothing. He was the back-up plan for every alpha who accepted problem shifters. He's famous for his skillset, but that skill is killing."

"Killing killers, Ben. Killing shifters who can't be saved and are murdering humans to fill some dark need. There's a difference between a serial killer and a man who was the arm of hard justice for our people. I thought you, of all people, would understand. You went through the shit, Ben. You lost your panther for years, lost your brother in Apex, lost your friends there, and you spiraled. I know that's why you picked me up and pushed me where I needed to be. You saw yourself in me. I see that in Logan. He's savable." She dragged in a long, shaking breath. "He's mine to save, do you understand?"

"Winter, maybe you should come home."

Warm tears streaked her cheeks. She shook her head. "Ben, he is home, and he's about to be annihilated by the dark dragon. I'll never have a home again."

She hung up the phone in a rush and dropped it in the grass. She couldn't take another second of him trying to convince her she was better off without the incredible feeling of safety Logan gave her.

He'd promised her day by day, and now the

choice was being taken away from both of them. And what could she do? She'd asked Ben to talk to Kane, but he'd refused to get on the wrong side of the dragon. And who was she? A submissive panther in a world of fire-breathers.

"You gonna join the crew?" Logan asked from right behind her.

Winter startled hard, gasping.

"Shhh," he said, trailing his fingers down the back of her bare neck. His eyes were the silver color of a minnow in the sun, and they were full of bottomless sorrow. Slowly, he drew the chains of the swing back, then released her and pushed her gently on her lower back.

Winter rested her cheek on the chain again and sighed, helped by kicking her legs. "I don't want you to go."

"Running won't do me any good. I did my research on Kane before I came here. He's ex special forces, survived God knows what on an elite team of shifters, and that was when he didn't even have his dragon. He has surveillance capabilities you wouldn't believe. In a matter of days, he found out about a kill that no one knew about but me and my old alpha. I wouldn't be able to crawl out from my rock for a single second for the rest of my life. That's a long time to live without making a mistake, and what kind of life would that be anyway? It wouldn't give me you."

"I could hide with you."

Logan huffed a breath. "Beauty," he murmured. "That's what you gave my life at the end, and I can't repay that gift by putting you in Kane's line of fire. The best way for me to protect you is to let you go."

Winter bit her lip hard so the sobbing sounds that crawled up the back of her throat wouldn't escape. "No," she whispered. "I can't join the Blackwing Crew."

"Why not?"

"You mean besides the fact the alpha is about to take the life of the man I love?"

"Don't say that. Don't talk about love, or it makes this harder."

"You're giving up. I didn't take you for a quitter."

"I quit a long time ago," Logan gritted out. He stopped pushing her and paced away like he would walk back up the street to the hotel. Running his hands through his hair, he circled back. "I hurt you. I hurt everyone who gets close. That's what I am,

Winter. You just aren't seeing me for what I am. Kane's doing a good thing. For the wrong reasons maybe, but this is what I've been asking for. I spent years trying to end it, and he's going to do it so I can go down fighting. I wish..."

"Say it."

A long snarl rattled his chest. "I wish I would've never met you so this could hurt less."

His words stole her breath away. Such poignant pain slashed through her heart that she nearly doubled over. "Take it back."

Logan shook his head for a long time, churning silver eyes locked on hers.

Winter stood and rushed him, shoved him hard in the chest so he felt the hurt that she did. "Take it back!"

"It would've been better for both of us if—"

Winter slammed her fists down against his chest. He didn't move, and it made her angrier so she did it again. Still no reaction, so she went to town beating on his torso, pushing him, sobbing until he slid his arms around her and pulled her against him. She struggled, but his body was a fortress. Sagging against him, Winter cried until the tears wouldn't come anymore.

And when she was spent, he folded her into his arms and strode back toward the motel. His cheeks were damp, too, so she knew he felt this. Knew he hadn't meant it, knew he was just trying to find a way to leave this world easier. But nothing inside her wanted to make this easy on him. She wanted to make it hard enough that he would come up with a way to save himself. Come up with a way to save *her*.

He didn't slow until he reached her room, 1010. He shoved open the door and dumped her on the bed, followed her down, and then his lips were on hers before the door even clicked closed. This kiss was fire. It was heat and desire, urgency and goodbye. Goodbye. She closed her eyes tight against the reality because it was too much. Winter slid her arms around his neck and pulled him closer, pushed her tongue past his lips and held on as he rolled her on top of him. His fingers shook as he tugged at her shirt, so she held his hands for a moment to steady him.

"It's okay to feel," she whispered. She didn't know why she said that, only that he needed to hear it. "Fuck the rest of the world, Logan. You can feel with me. I'll keep you safe."

His Adam's apple bobbed in his muscular throat as he swallowed hard. And then he cupped her neck and eased her to him gently. His lips were soft and steady. He didn't push his tongue in her mouth or suck her bottom lip. He just lay there under her, connected and frozen in this beautiful moment she wanted to stretch on forever and ever.

When he reached for her shirt again, his hands weren't shaking any longer, and the fire in his eyes had dimmed. Now he looked at her—*really* looked at her as he pushed her shirt upward and over her head. He unsnapped her bra and slid the straps down her arms slowly. Hooking a finger between the cups, he eased it off and sat up, pulled her to him, hand on her lower back.

When she arched upward, he drew one of her nipples into his mouth. There was no biting this time, only gentle, rhythmic sucking until she was rolling her hips with the pace he set. And then he moved to her other breast and gave it the same attention.

Needing to touch his skin, Winter pulled off his shirt and ran her hands down his chest. Logan stood, settled her feet on the floor, and then pushed her jeans down her legs, kneeling with them. He was unrushed, careful to put a steadying hand on her hip as he removed each shoe and sock, and then her jeans away from her ankles.

He kissed her stomach tenderly. Winter ran her fingers through his hair, angling his face up to hers. "You should say it once before you go."

"It'll make it harder on you."

"It'll make it harder if you leave me without saying it."

Logan buried his face against her stomach, hugged her tightly, there on his knees as though worshipping her. For a second, she didn't know if she could be strong enough to hear it. He felt it, though. She could tell by the way he looked at her, by the tears that had wet his cheeks earlier.

With a sigh, Logan tipped his chin up and trapped her in his gaze. "I love you, Winter Donovan. I take it back. I'm glad I met you. You were the best part of my life."

Her eyes burned again, but he didn't give her a chance to lose it. He stood, cupped her cheeks, and eased her backward, step by careful step toward the wall as he kissed her. It felt like dancing—another thing they would never get the chance to do.

When her back hit the wall, Logan slipped his tongue into her mouth, pressed his body along hers. His skin felt so good, as if he was made to hold her just like this.

This right here, in his arms, was her happy place.

Logan eased her panties down until they fell to her ankles. He unbuttoned his jeans and then kicked out of them as he continued kissing her soft, like saying *I love you* again but without words. He pulled the back of her knee up and settled her leg around him as he slid into her.

"Ooooh," she groaned as he filled her slowly.

There was no scent of fur, no snarl in his chest, no weight of dominance pressing against her shoulders. There was only her and Logan, as if his bear had curled up deep inside him to give them this—their last night.

Logan eased out of her and then back in until he pressed against her clit. He lowered his lips to her neck and worked her skin, right over the hickey he'd given her. This bruise he was giving her would last longer than him, and that thought killed her.

She rolled her hips, meeting him stroke for stroke as he sped up, his back flexing under her hands with his movement. She was trapped against the wall, and she'd never liked that in sex before, but she would give anything to stay trapped by Logan always. He didn't scare her anymore, not even a little.

Logan grunted and pushed into her faster. Pressure pulsed within her on every thrust. She was so close. Panting his name, she closed her eyes to the world and rode a wave of ecstasy only Logan could give her.

He clamped his teeth on her neck just how she liked and slammed into her deep, froze and shot warmth into her center, heating her from the inside out with each spurt of seed. Her orgasm exploded through her. Winter's body throbbed with pleasure as she raked her nails down his back.

Suddenly, Logan stopped moving within her, pulled her away from the wall, and just hugged her. He inhaled deeply and buried his face against her neck. He was shaking.

And now she was crying again. This shouldn't be the end.

It should've been their beautiful beginning instead.

SIXTEEN

Winter ran her fingertips across her lips as she watched Logan sleep. She was knelt beside the bed in the blue moonlight that filtered through the slats in the blinds. He'd slept here in her arms as a final gift, but she wasn't ready to quit. Not until he drew his last breath.

He was lying on his back, his face relaxed in his sleep, dark eyebrows smoothed out, dark lashes resting on his cheeks, jaw un-clenched. He looked like an angel fallen to earth. Perfect and scarless.

She was determined to change that, but she'd done this before.

Winter ran her fingers through her hair and gripped the base of her neck as she really considered this. She'd tried to save a sick man before and failed. She'd bit into Dad's forearm, and his response had been almost immediate. Blood had poured from the bite, poured from his mouth, from his eyes, from everywhere. He'd looked at her so scared, so confused, and all she could do was hold him as he died. Because of her.

This is different, her panther reasoned. *Logan is like us. He won't die. Not from our bite. We could save him, bind his bear to us even more, make him fight for his life...for us.*

Winter swallowed hard and tried to imagine biting him. She still remembered the feel and smell and taste from when she'd bitten Dad.

Could she even do that again?

To save Logan? Yes.

To make him want to fight? Yes.

Even if it was just her way of saying "I love you" back before he went? Yes.

She wanted him to be hers no matter what happened today. She needed him claimed if she was going to pull this off.

She had to do it fast, or he would yank away, so without thinking about it another moment, she lurched forward, grabbed his arm, and sank her teeth into the same place she'd bitten Dad. This time would be different. It had to be for her to be okay. For them both to be okay.

Logan flinched, and his eyes flew open, but he didn't move after that. He just watched her bite down as hard as she could. He didn't show pain, or anger. Instead, the corners of his lips curved up in a sad smile as she claimed him.

With a sob, she released his torn flesh and spat red onto the white sheets.

Logan held his bleeding arm out for her, and she crawled into the safe place he created, right against his ribs. She wiped her mouth on his skin, smearing crimson as a tear slipped from the corner of her eye. Logan's lips were pressed against her forehead, his hand stroking her hair.

"You love me, too," he whispered against her hairline.

Her voice would come out all weak and heartbroken if she spoke, so Winter nodded and cuddled closer.

"You're going to be okay, you know."

She didn't answer because he was wrong. Winter

had reached the peak of what one person could handle, and now she had nothing left to lose. She couldn't go back to Red Havoc, couldn't face Brody, couldn't join the Blackwings, couldn't do anything. She was stuck in purgatory until she knew Logan was safe again.

And a shifter with nothing to lose was the most dangerous creature on the planet.

Logan didn't know it yet, but today she would go up against the Blackwing Dragon himself as a panther doomed in a war she couldn't win against a fire-breathing dragon.

There was no other choice, though, because she couldn't sit by and let her mate burn to ashes.

****

Winter blew out a long breath before she got out of her truck. It was early, just at dawn, and the sky was still gray and not yet blue. Logan was still sleeping back at the motel, but Winter was in front of Kane's territory about to "yank the tail of the dragon," as Ben called it.

She hadn't bothered to clean all the dried blood from her mouth as she'd readied in the dark because Kane would need proof.

The hairs rose on her neck. *Careful*, her cat warned. Winter turned her head toward the woods and frowned at a flock of birds that sprung into the sky toward the east. The woods didn't feel right. Perhaps the dragons were out for an early morning walk or...something.

She narrowed her eyes at the silent woods before loping toward the front porch to get to the house faster. She didn't like the woods at her back right now, which made no sense because the woods were her most comfortable place.

Leaves rustled at the tree line, and Winter instinctively crouched on the porch, hissed long and loud.

The door behind her opened, and Rowan stood there in a baggy sweater and bell-bottom jeans. Her blond tresses were up in a messy bun that looked better than anything Winter could ever manage. Put-together, she may look, but her eyes were worried and darted to the woods, then back. To the woods, then back.

"What's wrong with this place?" Winter asked, scanning the woods.

"I don't know," Rowan whispered. "Kane and I

felt the same. He left a few minutes ago, but he hasn't returned. He told me to stay here."

Rowan smelled of fear, but why? She was a dragon. Clearly there was more to the Blackwing Second than Winter knew.

"You're bleeding," Rowan murmured as she came to stand beside Winter.

"It's not my blood. It's Logan's."

Rowan shot her a shocked look, but Winter had expected it and was already drawing up her shirt sleeve to show her the claw marks. "He's mine and I'm his. I can't join the Blackwings without him. I can't let Kane put him down."

Rowan shook her head. She looked pale, almost sick in the dawn light. "Well, now I can't either."

Hope bloomed inside of her chest. Rowan was her last hope at actually surviving Kane and saving Logan, too.

When Rowan frowned at the woods, Winter followed her gaze to Kane who was making his way out of the tree line. He looked odd, lurching this way and that, his soft brown eyes locked on his mate.

Behind him, the A-Team melted from the woods one at a time, appearing from behind trees like ghosts.

"Kane?" Rowan asked, panic tainting the word.

"R-Roe. Run," he slurred.

"What?" Rowan asked, stepping down the first stair.

"Run!" he yelled as he tripped and spun. When he hit the ground hard, Winter gasped. There were a dozen feather-tipped darts in his side, maybe more.

"Oh, my God," Rowan gasped, bolting for him. "Kane!"

Shit! Winter sprinted after her and yanked her back just as she reached Kane, but it was too late. Rowan's body jerked again and again. She turned in Winter's arms, her eyes wide and terrified. Now that her body was covered in darts, her eyes morphed from gold with elongated pupils to blue human eyes. Her dragon was going to sleep inside of her.

"No!" Winter yanked furiously at the darts to try and help her, but they were empty. "Rowan, Rowan, listen to me," she rushed out as the bright-eyed shifters breached the clearing. "Call them. Call them now before you lose her completely."

"Who?"

"The Bloodrunners and the D-Team." Winter

yanked Rowan's hair, arching her head back. "Do it, Rowan. I'll keep you and Kane alive until they get here."

Rowan rolled her eyes back in her head in a slow blink. "Don't leave us," she begged in a whisper.

The A-Team ran toward them, flooding from the woods like a violent tidal wave, yelling their war cries.

"I won't," Winter promised. "I need back-up though. Call for help."

Rowan clicked her firestarter and parted her lips. Winter angled her face away from the heat when Rowan blasted a fireball into the sky.

As Rowan went limp in her arms, Winter set her furious gaze on the closest attacker who had morphed into a tiger shifter.

Her animal roared to get out of her, and when Winter let the beast have her body, she released a hellish fury in a way she had never allowed her cat to have before. Because now she needed to kill. She needed to give into her predator instincts and bleed the assholes to survive. To protect the dragons.

She ran a few steps and leapt, clashing with the Bengal tiger.

And then, over the rush of rage and adrenaline and the deafening sound of roaring animals, there was pain.

SEVENTEEN

Kill them.

Logan startled awake. Breath ragged, he stared up at the ceiling of Winter's motel room. His bear was restless, and the edges of his vision were tinged in red. He only got like this when he was about to kill.

He sat up fast and scanned the room for Winter. God, let her be safe. Safe from me. Safe from...

Kill them.

Logan frowned and rubbed his hands over his eyes. A truck engine started up outside. He recognized it as Winter's. Old, wheezing engine that needed work. That truck was so her. She clung to things with a vice-like loyalty.

Logan padded to the window and pushed the

curtain aside just in time to see her driving away.

Hurry. Kill them.

Fuck, he really was losing his mind. Broken bear, broken Logan, but soon it would be all over. A vision of Winter mourning his death flashed across his mind. He hoped she would be okay.

Where was Winter going at the crack of dawn, and without waking him? Maybe she was leaving so she didn't have to say goodbye. He wasn't good at goodbyes either.

Her suitcase was open, her clothes scattered, but he'd memorized her things in the way he'd been trained to do. He had memorized every detail about this place, about his room, the office, the cars and license plates of the D-Team and the A-Team.

Fucking kill them.

Logan shook his head hard. Something felt wrong. Off. His skin rippled with gooseflesh, and he had the urge to move. To do something. Anything.

Desperate for a chore, he readied for the day in a rush and glared at his reflection in the mirror as he brushed his teeth. His eyes were the brightest he'd ever seen them, but why? Because today was his last day on earth? Maybe.

"No. Kill them," he growled around the toothbrush.

What the fuck, his bear could use him to talk?

"Logan, save her. She needs us."

All his hair lifted on his body. With only a moment of hesitation, Logan spat in the sink and rinsed as fast as he could. He grabbed his keys off the table and bolted out of the room.

Winter was going to see the dragons. She was going to plead for his life, or try to kill Dark Kane…something. He had to protect her from them. Fire, teeth, claws, ashes, ashes.

"Come on!" he yelled as his truck skidded around a turn.

The mountains were beautiful in the morning light, and he would've taken a moment to enjoy the last dawn of his life if there wasn't some bone-deep instinct telling him he was going to be too late.

Hurry.

"I'm fucking hurrying!"

Woods and rich greenery blurred by as he wound the mountain roads beside the snaking river. Almost there.

Kill them.

The dragons? God, how could he kill dragons?

But to protect our Winter?

Logan gripped the steering wheel so hard it bent under his grip. He had to keep his skin until he escaped the truck. He had to hold it together until he got to the dragons.

Through the thick tree canopy, a ball of fire shot up into the sky and exploded as it reached the clouds. A line of smoke was all that remained. Why would one of the dragon's blast a fireball up into the heavens? Unless…

Unless it was a call for help.

"Fuck!" Logan sailed down the steep entrance to Kane's land and over the bridge. He felt like he was going in slow motion. He gunned it up the last gravel hill and then slammed on the brakes when he hit the clearing.

What he saw made no sense. Two Bengal tigers were circling a battle, one white tiger lay on the ground, matted with red, staring vacantly. And in the center was a pair of grizzly bears, brawling, roaring, clawing at—oh, God.

A sleek black panther with ferocious gold eyes was fighting for her life. No, not just her life. She was poised over two limp bodies. She was crouched above Rowan and Kane, trying to keep the grizzlies from them. She slapped viciously, ripping into one of the bruin's necks. She was a weapon in motion, enraged, desperate. His loyal Winter was going to die for the dragons.

Logan slammed on the brakes and shoved the door open before he even put it in park.

Rage pumped through his veins as his bear ripped out of his skin.

Kill them. Kill them all.

He charged, every step fueled by hate and bloodlust. Winter was bleeding. He could smell it on the air. He could practically taste it, and for every drop of her blood they'd spilled, he would make them pay in agony.

One of the tigers hissed and leapt at him, but he swatted it away like it was nothing. A tree in the woods cracked loudly with the force of the asshole's body, but Logan was already focused on the next. He gave his back to the second tiger in desperation to rip the grizzlies off Winter. Pain raked down his back, but he didn't give a fuck about anything but the pitch black bear he'd zeroed in on. The one with his teeth deep in Winter's shoulder.

Logan barreled into the attackers, pulling them with him and away from Winter and the dragons. Everything smelled like blood. Winter had done good, hurt them, punished them, and now he would end them. Not cleanly, but like they deserved instead. Dishonorable deaths for dishonorable monsters. He raked his claws down the belly of one, spilling his guts and rendering him helpless. The next got a jugular shot, deep into the muscle, nearly severing his damn head so his shifter healing wouldn't work fast enough to fix him.

Logan's head was filled with the sounds of pain and the scent of blood and fur. He moved onto the next before one was expired because he knew the kill shots. He knew they were dying in piles behind him, one by one until there was a single wolf in the woods that remained. He had the bright green eyes of one of the A-Team. He turned to bolt, but fuck no to that. Logan chased him down, pounding his feet faster and faster behind him until he leapt on the back of the gray wolf. Logan snapped his neck in two, then shook his powerful head and tossed him into a pile of nothing on the ground. After the wolf's eyes dimmed with death, Logan stood on his hind legs and roared as long and as loud as he could to expel the rage still built up in his bloodstream.

****

When Logan's roar shattered the woods, Winter flinched from her pacing and lowered to her belly in fear. Oh, his bear was the monster she remembered, but even more terrifying. Now she truly believed his claim that he wouldn't have killed her. If he'd really wanted to, Logan could've ripped his truck apart panel by panel until she was in a bloody mound like the rest of the A-Team. The massacre had taken only seconds. Logan had been swift, skilled at killing. The last living grizzly, the black one who had ripped into her shoulder in an attempt to get to the dragons under her heaved one final breath and went still.

Logan had been so fast he'd blurred from one death blow to the next.

Rowan and Kane were bleeding from the claw marks Winter hadn't been able to protect them from. She needed to Change back so she could care for them, but the panther didn't want to give up her body yet.

Logan had saved her. He'd saved the dragons.

She wanted to meet his animal face-to-face in this braver body she had right now. The one with claws and teeth and weapons.

Logan lumbered from the woods, more massive than any grizzly she'd ever seen, wild or shifter. His chocolate-colored fur shook with each powerful step, and his long black claws dug into the earth as he strode toward her.

He. Felt. Terrifying.

Be brave. He's ours. He won't hurt us.

Crouching, she approached him slowly, but not directly. She slunk this way and that, keeping her neck exposed, but he didn't slow at all. In fact, he sped up. Would he charge? Would he kill her, too? Was he still wrapped up in the bloodlust she'd seen in his eyes when he'd single-handedly put down the A-Team? All but the white tiger. That kill was hers, and it would haunt her.

When Logan picked his pace up to a trot, she lowered to her belly and waited for him to eat her. He didn't, though. He stopped in front of her and ran his head down her side with such force, she toppled over.

If she could cry with joy and relief in this body, she would've. But all she had in her repertoire was a soft mewling sound as she pushed up on her hind legs and wrapped her paws around his neck. She extended her claws into his thick neck to steady herself and ran her tongue up his face, cleaning the blood, showing him the affection he deserved. She was still breathing because of him.

He wrapped a massive paw around her back and stilled, allowing her to clean the other side of his face. And when she was finished, he pressed his nose against the bite mark on her shoulder and the claw marks up her back. They would scar, but they weren't fatal. Already her shifter healing was working to cinch up her skin.

Everything hurt, but that was okay. She would rather feel pain than nothing. God, that had been so close.

Above them, a pair of raven shifters flew, and a great snowy owl circled up near the clouds. Three giant bear shifters loped out of the woods to the west, and suddenly, the sky was blotted out by an enormous green dragon with gold scales along her stomach. Harper and her Bloodrunners were here. She landed in the clearing, clicking her firestarter in warning as she circled Kane and Rowan's limp bodies, shaking the earth with each step. Logan roared his own warning to back the fuck off, and Winter crouched over their bodies protectively. She'd heard of the Bloodrunners, but she didn't know them, and right now, the Blackwing Dragons were at their most vulnerable. A black sports car pulled up, and Emma, Beast and Dustin piled out, looking around the clearing in shock and wariness.

Harper shrank into her human form. Straight-backed, naked, and furious, she glared at the piles of carnage in a trail that led to the woods. "Change back," she demanded.

Logan was pacing now, bumping Winter's side on each tight pass

"It's okay," Rowan whispered, her eyes wide. "Harper, they saved us."

A long horrifying rumble emanated from Kane, but his eyes were still closed, his breathing still steady. The air cracked with dark power that hurt Winter's stomach, and Kane's skin cracked on his arms, then cinched together, then cracked again wider, like his dragon would force his way out of him at any moment. Whatever was happening inside of Dark Kane was bad.

Winter Changed back in a rush, and behind her, Logan tucked his bear away, too.

Harper knelt down near Rowan and lifted her head in her lap. "What happened?"

"The A-Team... They weren't here to join our crew. They were here to end it." Rowan was shaking badly, from the meds or from adrenaline, or maybe both. A tear slipped from her eye as she rolled her head and looked at her mate. "They put our dragons to sleep. Harper, The Darkness doesn't like being put to sleep. Not after being dormant for so long. Everyone needs to leave."

"The Darkness?" Dustin asked, his eyes glowing as he paced, gaze locked on Kane. He was snarling, like he wanted to attack. "He calls his dragon The fucking Darkness?"

"Get in the car," Beast told Emma.

When Dustin stayed, glaring at Kane's limp body, Beast grabbed him by the scruff of the neck and shoved him toward the car.

"What about you?" Winter asked Rowan in a worried whisper. "Will he hurt you?"

"No," she said. "But I'm the only one who can keep The Darkness from burning the mountains again. Winter, thank you for staying. For fighting. For keeping us safe."

Winter looked at the claw marks on Rowan's arms and shook her head, disappointed in herself for not being better, bigger, more dominant. Rowan would have scars like her now.

"Go on," Rowan said. "Kane will be eating ashes today, and I don't want any of you around when he does."

Winter looked up at Harper and backed away, exposing her neck. And when she reached Logan, Winter slipped her hand into his offered one. He'd been silent except for the constant growl in his throat. All Winter could feel was his bear.

"See you soon, Rowan," Winter promised over her shoulder.

"Winter," Rowan called weakly, stopping them in their tracks.

"Yeah?" Winter asked, turning.

"My friends call me Roe."

Winter smiled and swallowed down the thick emotion in her throat. "See you soon, Roe."

EIGHTEEN

Kane's Mountains smelled like fresh soot and smoke. The wind whipped Winter's hair around as she stood near a long scorch mark where Logan had dropped the A-Team two days ago.

Two days? It felt like so much longer. Winter cuddled her jacket closer. All of the worrying and the nightmares over killing that tiger shifter made every minute feel like ten. She'd stopped trying to sleep completely, but that hadn't lifted the concerns over Kane's threat.

He could still kill Logan.

Logan slipped his strong hands over her shoulders and kissed the back of her head. "You ready?" he murmured against her hair.

"Why do you think he only called us here?" she asked in a whisper.

"Come on now, you aren't a scaredy cat, are you? I saw you, little brawler, going to war with grizzlies and tigers to protect dragons. You turn killer when someone you care about is threatened. Everything is going to be okay." But his voice wavered on that last part.

Winter turned and kissed his knuckles, then let him lead her to Kane's cabin. Logan knocked so hard the door rattled, but that was just him. Big, dominant man who didn't know his own strength sometimes. Except with her. He turned gentle when he touched her.

"Come in," Kane clipped out.

Logan pushed the door open and stepped aside, allowing Winter in first.

Rowan and Kane sat at the kitchen table facing them with a pair of blue folders in front of them. When Kane had invited her to be a part of the crew, he'd pulled her registration papers from one just like those.

Winter inhaled sharply with hope.

Roe was smiling, and her eyes were dancing like

she couldn't wait to spill secrets.

"Have a seat," Kane murmured.

Logan pulled out Winter's seat for her, then took his own right beside her. He took a deep inhale and rested his palm on Winter's thigh under the table to help steady her. Or perhaps he was trying to steady himself. He'd been touching her a lot over the last couple of days. Touching her, holding her hand, stroking her hair, brushing her cheek, neck, shoulder... It all seemed to settle his bear.

"Ben called me," Kane said low as he fingered one of the folders. "He asked me a favor. He asked that I spare Logan's life, and he said he thought in doing so, I would be sparing your life." He lifted dragon green eyes to Winter and gave her a small smile. "I know the feeling, Winter. I know what that mark on Logan's arm means, and I know what you asked my mate. You're bonded, as I'm bonded to Rowan, and the thought of losing your other half is unbearable. Am I close?"

Dipping her emotional gaze to the table, Winter nodded. "He's mine to protect."

"Is she yours to protect?" Kane asked Logan.

"Yes."

Rowan shoved a folder toward her. "Winter, you already have your invite to the crew. Here is the rest of what you need. And a gift."

Kane said softly, "The gift isn't much, but it's a big deal for me."

Winter opened the folder where there was another copy of crew registration paperwork, as well as mobile home options. One was a singlewide trailer with a porch and wooden shingles covering the outside. It looked homey. The other was a doublewide trailer that looked just the same, only bigger. And stuffed into a clear plastic sleeve in the center was a black keychain. It had a bear paw cut-out.

"Is this a bottle opener?" Winter asked, plucking it from the folder. It had an inscription. *Blackwing Crew.*

"We have matching ones," Rowan said excitedly.

"Look, I didn't want to be an alpha," Kane said, frowning. "I know I was hard on you, but look at what the A-Team did. They almost ended my mate's life." He didn't mention his own, like it didn't matter. "The rest of the D-Team is still under consideration, but I'm not ready to pull the trigger on anyone but you two. Winter, you stood over us and took blow after blow just to keep us breathing. And Logan, you came in and saved us all. That's the kind of loyalty I want in my mountains. I thought I could just get away with it being Rowan and me for always and fuck the world, you know? But it seems a crew would offer us protection I didn't realize we needed. And also friendship. Rowan needs that, and maybe so do I." Kane cleared his throat and flicked the other folder across the table to Logan.

Logan looked completely stunned. Slowly, he opened the folder, and there was a copy of registration paperwork, the same mobile home plans, and the same keychain.

Winter's face crumpled, and her eyes burned with tears. In this moment, it felt like all of the dreams she didn't even realize she had were coming true. "You won't kill him then?" she asked in a broken voice.

"Never." Kane leveled Logan with a look. "Do you understand? Never will I, or my mate, kill you. If you join my crew, you try. You get steady. You gain control of your bear, and no excuses either, because I know what it takes to get a monster back under control. It's hard every day, but Rowan keeps me fighting." Kane tipped his head toward Winter. "Let your mate keep you fighting, too. Sign that paperwork, and you will be agreeing to never bring up an honorable death again. It's an oath to keep going, and to own your life again. I don't give a shit about temporary crew members. I care about the future of my mountains, of my make-shift family. I care that you and Winter will be there for our future children as they grow up. I care about being there for your future cubs. I care about building a community I can depend on. I haven't had that before." Kane blew out a steadying breath. "Winter Donovan, do you accept our terms?"

How could she not? How could she turn down such a beautiful promise? No longer would she be Winter of Nowhere. From here on, she would be Winter of the Blackwing Crew. She would have a home, a family, a steady future, and most importantly, she would have Logan by her side for always. "Yes, Alpha. I would be honored to be a Blackwing."

"And you, Logan Furrow?" Kane asked. "Do you accept our terms?"

Logan was watching Winter, his eyes so full of emotion it threatened to overwhelm her. "Day by day?" he asked her softly.

Winter melted against his side, right under his arm where he always made her feel safe and warm. She couldn't stop the tears from rolling down her cheeks. "Day by day."

Logan swallowed hard and dragged his silver gaze to Kane. "Yes, Alpha."

A slow smile stretched Kane's face. "Logan and Winter, welcome to the Blackwing Crew."

BLACKWING DEFENDER

Want more of these characters?

Blackwing Defender is the first book in a three book series based in Kane's Mountains.

Check out these other books from T. S. Joyce.

Blackwing Wolf
(Kane's Mountains, Book 2)

Blackwing Beast
(Kane's Mountains, Book 3)

Also, if you would like to read Kane and Rowan's story, it can be found in the final book of the Harper's Mountains series.

Blackwing Dragon
(Harper's Mountains, Book 5)

About the Author

T.S. Joyce is devoted to bringing hot shifter romances to readers. Hungry alpha males are her calling card, and the wilder the men, the more she'll make them pour their hearts out. She werebear swears there'll be no swooning heroines in her books. It takes tough-as-nails women to handle her shifters.

Experienced at handling an alpha male of her own, she lives in a tiny town, outside of a tiny city, and devotes her life to writing big stories. Foodie, wolf whisperer, ninja, thief of tiny bottles of awesome smelling hotel shampoo, nap connoisseur, movie fanatic, and zombie slayer, and most of this bio is true.

Bear Shifters? Check

Smoldering Alpha Hotness? Double Check

Sexy Scenes? Fasten up your girdles, ladies and gents, it's gonna to be a wild ride.

For more information on T. S. Joyce's work,
visit her website at
www.tsjoyce.com

Printed in Great Britain
by Amazon